P9-DHL-500

When *USA TODAY* bestselling author **Terri Brisbin** is
not being a glamorous romance author or in a deadline-
writing-binge-o-mania, she's a wife, mom, grandmom
and dental hygienist in the southern New Jersey area.
A three-time RWA RITA® Award finalist, Terri has had
more than forty-five historical and paranormal romance
novels, novellas and short stories published since 1998.
You can visit her website, www.terribrisbin.com, to learn
more about her.

Visit the Author Profile page
at Harlequin.com for more titles.

I met James Townsley in November 2021. We were introduced by friends because he was Scottish and I, well, I love and write about Scotland, and so we spent hours chatting that day in November. James had moved to Canada from southwestern Scotland after World War II and then down into the US, where he settled in the New York City/New Jersey area. He wanted to hear about my recent story that was set where he grew up and I had questions... so many questions for him.

James moved home to Scotland the week after we met and I've just learned he recently passed away.

So, I dedicate this story to him—a kind and dear man who had so many adventures in his life and gave me such inspiration to write this story. I'm glad you got home, James.

Prologue

Village of Achnacarry, Scotland—
the year of our Lord 1377

Iain Mackenzie watched her approach and saw the truth in the way she moved and in the sad gaze in her eyes before she spoke a word. When Glynnis finally met his eyes, he hated the message there. She turned her gaze from his as she made her way along the path that divided his mother's neat garden into smaller sections. Standing as she reached him, Iain held out his hand, wondering now if she would accept his touch.

Her smaller hand slipped into his, entwining her fingers with his, and he savoured this moment, fearing it would be the last time for such intimacy.

'So, 'tis—' he said.

'You have heard—' she started to say and instead shook her head. 'Go on, Iain.'

'You are summoned home then?' He already knew the answer, but asked anyway. To gauge her response, her willingness or not, to be given in marriage to a man she did not know.

'On the morrow, it seems.' Her answer came out as a whisper as she tightened her grasp on his hand. Iain pulled her down to sit with him on the stone bench.

'So soon? When he only sent word a few days ago?' Iain felt the noose of regret tightening around his neck. If only…

'My father sent word only when all the arrangements were made.'

He took in a breath, gathered his courage and spoke. Words he should have said before. Words he knew in his heart to be true. Words that could not be unspoken once he said them to her.

'Marry me, Glynnis.' She gasped and blinked in surprise. 'Do not return home. Stay here and marry me.'

'Iain, you ken that is impossible. I must marry whomever my father commands me to.'

'Nothing is impossible if we want it, Glynnis.' He stood and paced before her, slowly, several times back and forth before nodding. 'Look at my cousin's actions. He chose love over all the rest.'

Their situation was not exactly the same, for his cousin Robbie had indeed married the woman his father had intended. But the consequences of their actions had impacted the very future and stability of the Clan Cameron.

'Iain, this is different. We are different.' She reached out to him this time and he pulled her to her feet and into his embrace.

Desperation rose within him and he wanted to

scream out his frustration and fury over losing her. For he would, he would lose her. Resignation filled her eyes and even the slump of her shoulders cried it out to him.

'Just tell me, Glynnis. Tell me if you would marry me. If I could convince your father,' he said, 'would you marry me?'

She did not need to say a word. The tears streaming from her eyes said it all. Iain lifted her chin and kissed those tears on her cheeks. He touched his lips to hers and waited for her to open to him. He tasted her tongue against his and the saltiness of her tears for the last time.

'I love you, Iain,' she whispered against his mouth as she lifted her face away.

Stepping back, he watched as she assumed the façade she showed to everyone else. The gracious gentle lady with an ever-present smile and nod. The dutiful, obedient daughter who never questioned her father's rule. The perfect woman that every nobleman needed as a wife. And he knew, without a doubt, that she would become that to the man she married.

But he knew the real Glynnis beneath that disguise. He'd seen the cracks that had exposed the woman who lived with the doubts and fears and needs that assailed everyone. No matter their class or position or birth. The Glynnis she presented to the world was too far above him, with his bastard birth, his youth and his lack of connections. That Glynnis could never be his.

Iain did not vent his anger at her, for she was not the one behind this. With nothing else to say, he kissed her gently once more and released her, putting a full pace between them.

'I wish you much happiness in your marriage, Glynnis.' Disbelief shone as she watched him. 'I do, love,' he said. 'I would never want anything but the best for you, even if it cannot be with me.'

It was over. He stood no chance of being a man who could claim her against her father's will and plans. And he had no intention of punishing her with his anger and impotence over that sad fact. He slipped a small, wooden figurine of a horse he'd carved into her hand.

Iain did not wait for her to leave, for she would want to gather her control and wipe away her tears before allowing anyone to see them. The only times he'd seen her lose that perfect control had been in his company or in his arms. He turned and walked away, counting every step and praying with every part of him that she would speak his name. That she would stop him and accept his offer. That she would take the risk that he was and be something other than the obedient daughter she'd been raised to be.

Iain was on the path outside his mother's house before he stopped hoping.

He did not join the chieftain and his family for their evening meal that night. He did not sleep at all, but instead found a place on the battlements and stared out into the darkness. And when morning came and the small group gathered in the yard below him, he watched her leave.

Three weeks later...

The darkness swirled around him, interrupted some-how by a voice. As Iain swam up through the turmoil, his head pounded and his stomach burned. Even open-ing his eyes did no good against the confusion and gut-wrenching waves of the nausea that resulted from drinking too much ale. He struggled to turn over and to get away from the increasing light, but he could not.

'Iain!' the voice yelled.

He could have let himself sink back into the dark-ness and he would have, except for the deluge of icy water that followed the call. Screaming as he pushed to his feet, he found his stepfather standing there holding an empty bucket.

'Davidh!' he yelled as he gathered his sopping hair and shoved it out of his face. 'What is going on?'

It took little time for the change in position to wreak havoc with the way his belly felt and he stum-bled a few paces away from Davidh and emptied the meagre contents into the rough grass there. He took several breaths before he noticed that Davidh held out a skin to him.

'Wash out your mouth.'

He did as he was told and could hear the anger in his stepfather's tone. Nay, not anger as much as dis-appointment. And, by God, he hated hearing that. Sitting back on his heels, he spat out the last of the water and wiped his mouth with the back of his hand.

'Walk with me, Iain.'

Only then did Iain look around to see where he was. He did not remember seeking out this place. The sound of the rushing water nearby was unmistakable—somehow, even in a drunken stupor, he'd made his way up the dangerous path alongside the two-level waterfall to the clearing above it. A path that had been the location of many accidents and injuries.

It mattered not that he'd learned the way as a child. It mattered not that he and his mother had lived here before she'd married Davidh. Anyone who did not have a care in climbing the hidden path around the powerful currents and slick rocks risked death or losing a limb. And yet, here he was, without any memory of how he'd made it up.

He followed Davidh into the small cottage in the clearing and sat across the table from him. Iain might have acted a fool lately, but he was not one and he had a clear idea of what Davidh would say. It was only a matter of time before he faced a reckoning for his behaviour since…Glynnis left.

'Do you remember last night at all?' Davidh asked. Iain shook his head. 'Do you remember laying waste to the chieftain's personal supply of *uisge beatha* given him by The MacLerie? Or the insults thrown at him and others at his table?'

Iain's stomach sank now for a different reason than his overindulgence. He'd been nothing if not welcomed by a man who could have as easily ordered his death as a possible threat to his own sons' claims to his position. Others might have done that. Others had done as much. Robert Cameron had given him a place as the grandson of Robert's eldest brother and previous chieftain. Bastard though he was, he and his mother had been offered a hand and protection by Robert when they needed it most.

'I am sor—'

'Your apology is not to me, Iain, so do not waste your words or efforts. You must make it right with Robert.' Davidh stood and walked to the door. Easing it open a scant few inches, he stared towards the edge of the falls. 'I ken how much you miss the lass, but the truth is that she was never for you. When she did not marry Robbie, her father betrothed her to marry The Campbell's son.' Turning back, he crossed his arms over his chest and his gaze turned hard.

'But truth be told, Iain, you were not worthy of her.'

Iain had never heard his worst fears spoken aloud and it was shocking to hear them from Davidh now. 'What?'

'Bastard-born, not trained or interested in leading the clan, no experience in anything but woodworking and riding. Your skills in reading and numbers are not what a chieftain needs even in his clerk. Her father would never have considered an offer for her hand in marriage to a man—nay, a lad like you.'

Iain jumped to his feet and crossed the small space without thinking.

'Her father would have been insulted by an offer from someone such as you. And no one of his position would blame him.' Davidh opened the door and stepped outside. 'She is too high above you.'

Iain's vision went blurry with rage and he shoved Davidh, knocking him to the ground and punching him over and over. No matter how he punched, Davidh turned his blows aside. Rolling to his feet, he pushed Iain away and shook his head.

'You cannot even fight well,' Davidh said, while motioning him to come at him. 'Of course you are not worthy.'

Like his actions of the night before, Iain lost track of everything but his anger and his pain at the truth in Davidh's words. Relentlessly, he poured it out at Davidh, punching, kicking, shoving the man until Iain could not breathe. Falling to his knees, he dragged in loud gasps. With his hands on his legs to steady him, it took a long time before he could lift his head. Davidh stood a few paces away watching him, looking uninjured and not even winded. Davidh walked to him and crouched down to meet his gaze.

'Losing her hurts. I ken how it feels to lose someone you love, Iain. But how you deal with it, how you move forward from this day, is what matters now. You can choose to remain as you are or you can choose to claim a future that you would have had if your true father had lived.' Davidh had been his father Malcolm Cameron's closest friend.

'I am all those things you said—bastard, unworthy, ill-equipped,' Iain said in defeat. Davidh stood.

'And you are yet young and untrained. With great effort, you could rise to become a man who has the choices. Who can control his life. Who could be the one making the decisions.' His gaze narrowed and his voice lowered. 'Who could choose love.'

'What?' Iain said, rising to stand. He pushed his hair out of his eyes and dusted off some of the dirt he was now covered in. 'How?'

'Simple. Claim your father's place.'

'Simple? That's daft, Davidh.'

'Daft? Aye, unless you are willing to risk everything to do it. To do what is necessary. To give up the lack of control and temper that guides your actions now.' His stepfather held out his hand. 'Well, Iain. Will you? Will you claim your father's place and be the man he would have wanted you to be?'

Could he do it?

Davidh's words were not the first time his stepfather had tried to warn him about his life. Nor the first time he'd thought about what and where he could be.

Her loss made the necessity of change clear to him. Iain no longer wished to be the one left behind. The one who had no power. The one who couldn't choose his path, his life. Iain would never have Glynnis and he would mourn that loss every day. He would remember her every time he carved a new piece of wood. He would think of her every time he sat at table in the hall of Achnacarry Castle. But he would not allow it—the powerlessness—to happen to him again.

He would not.

Iain rose to his full height and accepted his stepfather's hand and the offer behind the gesture.

And he never looked back.

Chapter One

Three years later...

Glynnis MacLachlan took one more look around the large chamber she'd called hers for these last three years before walking out into the corridor and closing the door. Her maid stood waiting for her and they walked in silence down the stairs to the hall below. Maggie was the only person who'd arrived with her and she'd be the only one returning with her to her father's holding.

No one, not a single servant or any kin of her dead husband, spoke to her as she passed them. Not a word of farewell or good wishes was offered. The only sound breaking into the silence was that of her boots as she walked the long path across the stone floors to the doorway of the keep. Glynnis nodded at the servant who opened the door and let out a breath that she'd been holding.

Her husband's brother met her there and nodded to the waiting escort that would see her...home. Truly, though, in this moment, she had no place she would call home. Years spent at Achnacarry preparing for a wedding that never happened. Three years here with nothing but a broken body and spirit to show for it. Now? Now, she would go where her father ordered when he decided her future.

'We received word from Lady Cameron, Glynnis,' Gillespie Campbell said. Holding out his arm to her, he guided her down the steps to the travel party and the horse awaiting her. 'She welcomes you to visit her while you are…recovering from your loss.'

Such polite words for losing a husband and a child within hours of each other. Such a mild way to explain the destruction of her soul and her heart and, especially, her life. The invitation from Lady Elizabeth would give her a respite before facing her father when he returned from his journey to his lands in England.

The last time she'd been there as a foster daughter, learning the skills and tasks she would need as the wife of the clan's heirs, she'd lived in the keep as the family did. This time, Lady Elizabeth assured her of a place away from the centre of things—a small cottage where she could be on her own until she could face…anyone.

Glynnis allowed Gillespie's help in mounting and she gathered the reins in her hands while her maid gained her own seat. She nodded at Martainn's brother.

'The men have been ordered to journey at an easy pace, to accommodate your…condition. Tell Douglas if you have need of anything.'

'My thanks, Gillespie, for seeing to these arrangements.'

'Glynnis, I—' He stopped himself and shook his head. 'I wish you safe travels.'

Clearly, he had something more or different to say, but kept the words behind his teeth. Glynnis shook the reins and touched her knees to her mount and began the journey south. She waited for the inevitable pain to tear her apart as she passed through the gates and on to the road. And for the need to turn back and watch the keep grow further away. Or she waited for tears to fall as she recalled the memories of the last three years here, with its challenges and brief successes and so many losses and failures.

Yet each mile brought only distance and the great emptiness within her held no emotions at all. For she had cried out all the tears she had in these last few years and sobbed out every bit of pain and loss until there was nothing left.

Nothing but the yawning darkness where her heart and soul should be.

The journey had passed by in a vague haze and several days later, Glynnis and her maid stood before a small cottage on the edges of the land surrounding Achnacarry Castle. Lady Elizabeth had found a place for her that was away from the main road to the village and deep in the forest. Her nearest neighbour was the mill that sat beside a branch off the River Arkaig as it made its way from Loch Arkaig to Loch Lochy, the strong current providing power for the millstone.

Quiet. Away from people. Away from responsibility. Away from…life. For the first time, Glynnis answered to no one. It would not be for long, but she would take every moment she could.

Maggie set things to rights in a short while, for the cottage was simple and not even as large as her chamber in the keep had been here all those years ago. Her maid, a cousin sent along with Glynnis to her Campbell marriage, had asked to accompany her to Achnacarry. With her calm demeanour and skill at seeing to Glynnis's needs without question or judgement, Maggie seemed the perfect companion. It also helped that she was not too young a lass or given to idle chatter— something Glynnis did not have the strength to do or to tolerate at this time.

Over the next few days, Lady Elizabeth sent messages and food to the cottage, asking after her newly arrived *cousin* Clara—a name they'd chosen to avoid knowledge of her in the clan—but otherwise she made no demands of her. One morning, a lad appeared at her door and said that he was there to do the heavier tasks and help Maggie as she might need. By the end of that day, the woodpile and the supply of cut peat reached nigh to her shoulders, the barrel of water stood full and the jars of flour and oats and other foodstuffs were ready for any cooking she or Maggie might do.

One day bled into the next as she tried and failed to do anything but sit and watch her efficient servant in her tasks. It was not that she was busy planning her future or even contemplating her past. Nay, the hours drifted by her without thoughts or words forming inside her mind. Though Maggie informed her of Lady Elizabeth's generosity and carefulness in providing for them, Glynnis ate little of their bounty and spent countless hours in dreamless, restless slumber.

It was the morn when the storms that had controlled the skies above for a long while, mayhap several days even, ended and she noticed something had changed. Her exhaustion had lifted and a restless sense began to fill part of her emptiness. Maggie, bless her, was ever watchful and must have seen something, for the maid began handing her a sewing needle, lengths of thread and garments and such that needed repairs.

Two more days had passed before Glynnis realised that she did not recognise the clothing or other items. And another before she thought to ask about them.

'Maggie?'

'My lady?' the maid replied, pausing in her own work to meet her gaze. Glynnis saw the surprise there.

'Whose garments are these?' Glynnis held up a small tunic of coarse wool before her.

'I think that is for the miller's youngest bairn, my lady.'

'The miller?'

Maggie's brow furrowed but she did not hesitate. 'Aye, my lady. The miller—James—and his family live next to the mill. His son came by some days ago and checks in to see if we need help.'

Glynnis remembered the tall, muscular lad, but nothing else came to mind. 'Have I spoken to him?'

'Aye, my lady. He is called Edward,' Maggie said.

Only because she was studying her maid's face did she see the faint blush creep up into the younger woman's cheeks. At a different time that would have been an interesting reaction.

'I do not remember.' Little of what had happened since she had mounted the horse that brought her here. And, if truth be told, much of the last weeks was all a blur.

'He will be here later to see to the horses and bring fresh water.' So, her maid kenned the lad's schedule?

'And to collect the mending?' Glynnis asked.

'My lady, I—' Maggie stuttered a few words before speaking clearly. 'I had nothing to do once everything was put away here and you were...*resting*. My mum always told me to keep myself busy or risk tempting the devil, so I...'

'Offered to help the miller's wife with her chores?' Maggie nodded, uncertainty filling her eyes. 'I take no issue with you helping those who are helping us, Maggie.' She glanced at the pile of garments in the basket beside her and only then realised how many they'd mended. 'So, a son and another?'

'And two more in between those.' Her colour rose as she revealed that she knew more about the family.

When Glynnis turned her attention to sewing the torn edge of the tunic on her lap, they fell back into companionable silence. A wave of exhaustion passed through her. The words they'd just exchanged, as short a conversation as it was, used up whatever strength she'd saved. It was just that and had nothing to do with the talk of bairns, or their garments. Handing the finished repair to Maggie, Glynnis leaned her head against the high wooden back of the chair.

'Ye look peaked, my lady. Should ye rest a bit?'

Torn between the need to escape into the shadows of sleep and the growing restless urge, Glynnis shook her head and stood.

'Nay,' she said, walking across the cottage to the door. Lifting the latch and tugging it open to judge the fairness of the swirling winds, Glynnis looked back over her shoulder. 'I will spend a few minutes outside, I think.'

When Maggie put her sewing aside, Glynnis waved her off and stepped out. She pulled the door behind her and stood still, letting the breezes flow over her. It was a mild day in late spring in the Highlands, surprising considering the storms of late and that most any day here could go from the warmest summer-like weather to a wintry chill in only hours. Deciding she needed no cloak, Glynnis strode a few paces from the cottage and looked about.

Her arrival here days—or could it be more than a week?—ago was lost in a haze of confused memories. She'd not stepped outside the safety and refuge of the small haven granted her by Lady Elizabeth until now. Slowly and carefully, she walked around the cottage, observing the small, fenced-in area where their horses grazed. Their hay and feed lay close to the stone wall and under a canopy of canvas to keep it dry.

As she regained her bearings from her years here in Achnacarry and the position of the sun overhead, she listened for the sound of water and followed it. Though the river that it fed was stronger, the rushing stream ahead of her was the perfect size and position and strength to service the mill. Reaching the edge of it, she knew the mill was off to the west a bit, close enough to walk to, but not close enough to see or hear. To her right, to the east, the stream joined the river and flowed into the loch. For now, she stood there, listening to the water and letting the sun's light warm her even among the trees' cover.

Had she ever been at this kind of leisure before in the whole of her life? Picking up a long stick, she dipped it into the swirling water near her feet and drew meaningless shapes on the surface. Every moment of her years on earth, she'd been someone's daughter or someone's betrothed. Someone's wife. Someone's mother, if only for minutes. And now she was someone's widow. Nay, she had never been on her own and it was an unnerving sensation to stand here with no demands on her time or her skills.

Glynnis stood in the quiet for a short while longer until the distant sound of riders echoed from the road leading to the mill, breaking into her melancholy reverie. She let the stick drop on to the bank of the stream and made her way back to the cottage. As she lifted the latch, she made the first decision in a long time.

On the morrow, she would walk to the mill and back.

Even though her body ached from this little activity and its recent malaise, she would do it.

Iain stood next to his stepfather, watching a situation he did not remember ever seeing before. Oh, he knew that no marriage could run smoothly all the time, but he never expected to witness his chieftain and his wife arguing in the middle of the hall.

In front of others.

Waves of discomfort rolled off his stepfather, The Cameron's commander. And yet no one there seemed to know what to do…except look away until the couple finished. Though their voices were not raised in anger, their expressions made it clear—Robert and Elizabeth Cameron were not in agreement over some matter.

'Are we here earlier than he expected us?' Iain asked in a low voice. 'Mayhap they did not realise we were coming?'

'Nay, Iain. 'Twas Robert's own summons that brought us here now. I suspect the lady did not ken.'

Iain noticed as Davidh caught the eye of the steward. Struan stood closer to the couple, and, at Davidh's nod, he approached them slowly. Iain followed Davidh's lead and turned slightly away. Crossing his arms over his chest, he leaned in.

'I ken I have only been here nine years now, but I cannot ever remember them disagreeing over anything of substance before.' Had they argued over food or the colour of the tapestries on the wall? Aye. And on other small matters or questions? Aye. But never on matters of substance and on display like this. 'Do you think this is about the betrothal?'

Davidh glanced over his shoulder at the still-whispering couple and shook his head.

'Nay. The lady has been quite clear and vocal in her support of this arrangement for you, Iain. 'Tis not about that, I am certain.'

Struan managed to interrupt them somehow and

they watched as the two took a pace away from each other and nodded. The lady turned to leave, but stopped. She shook her head, closed her eyes and lifted her face up, as if offering a prayer to the Almighty. Lady Elizabeth had taken a few steps away when the chieftain spoke her name loud enough for all to hear. Her hesitation in facing him made Iain think she meant to ignore his call, but the lady turned back.

'I fear this will not end well, Elizabeth. Not well at all.'

The chieftain's voice was filled with a mix of sorrow and resolve and the sound of it made Iain's stomach tighten. This did not bode well—not for the laird, the lady or anyone here at Achnacarry. With one glance at those who yet stood watching in awkward silence, Robert Cameron cleared the hall of those who should be about their duties. In that moment, Iain wished *he* had another place to be.

Davidh tapped his arm and Iain walked with him up to Robert, wondering at the summons and whether the argument they'd witnessed was connected. They followed Robert's motion to follow and made their way into a smaller chamber connected to the large hall where the chieftain saw to private matters. A servant entered behind them and placed a jug of ale and cups for them on the table. They sat, and after drinking a good portion of the ale in his cup, Robert let out a breath and nodded.

'Word has come from the King and he is amenable to a match that will link our families,' he said. Now pride filled his words, for the coming betrothal would result in an increase in power and make the

Camerons one of the most important clans in Scotland. 'Before I move forward with this, Iain, I need your assurance you are ready.' Robert looked first at him and then at Davidh.

''Tis a great honour, my lord.'

'Aye,' Davidh added. 'A great honour for the Camerons and my stepson as well.'

'This is about more than just the marriage, Iain. You are not the lad you were on your arrival or even the same as the one who stepped in when Robbie made his choice. But my question is—' The chieftain stood and held out his arm to Iain. 'Are you now the man who will accept this place, the one your father held during his life, as tanist of the Clan Cameron?'

Davidh stood and positioned himself behind Iain—at his back as always, but especially as he'd been these last three years of gruelling training, hard lessons learned and endless hours of struggling to accomplish his goal. Meeting Robert's steely gaze, Iain grasped his chieftain's hand.

'If you believe me ready, I am your man, my lord,' Iain said. 'I will serve you and my clan as my father would have wanted me to.'

Robert pulled him in and hugged him before releasing. 'Ready? Aye, you are. But there is yet plenty of time to continue to prepare.' Stepping away, Robert took up the jug and filled their cups once more.

'Mo Righ's, mo Dhuchaich.' Robert held his cup aloft and spoke the clan's motto, which seemed to be so appropriate in this moment. *For King, for Country.* Iain and Davidh repeated their leader's words before they emptied their cups and slammed them

on the wooden table. 'I will be asking the elders for official approval, but they have each stated their support of you, Iain.'

'Are you certain that Tomas will not stake his claim? Or that Robbie will not pursue it after all?' he asked. He wanted it all made clear.

With the custom of the next male in a line, usually the chieftain's son, inheriting the high seat and control over their lands and wealth becoming more prevalent in even the Highland clans, any of the laird's sons would have first claim. Alan Cameron, whom Robert accepted as his own, had taken himself out of consideration by his equal claim —by blood and loyalty—to the Mackintosh clan. Though Iain's claim through his long-dead father, who had been in line to inherit from his own father, was acknowledged, the fact that Iain's parents had never married would lessen his support—if one of his other two cousins chose to claim their right.

'Robbie is content where he is—as is Sheena,' Robert said. 'He serves by overseeing the southern holdings and is close enough to satisfy his mother's need to be near their children.' A fleeting darkening of his gaze at the mention of the lady was gone before the laird continued, 'Tomas is competent, but has not the drive.' 'Twas not an insult to his son, for even Iain realised it was a fair assessment of his cousin.

Robbie had given up his claim and chosen the love of his life instead. Sheena would never have been able to manage the demands of being a chieftain's wife and Robbie understood that forcing her to that would destroy her. And his cousin loved his wife too much to consider doing that.

'There will be a ceremony when you take your place and afterwards I will begin formal negotiations for the betrothal,' the chieftain said as he walked to the door and lifted the latch. 'But the deed is as good as done in my mind and in the King's. It will be a time of celebration, Iain. Davidh, you should be proud.'

'I am, my lord,' his stepfather said. 'His mother will be...'

'Overjoyed, I am certain. Iain, I ken how important it will be to her, since she came here as an outsider, not expecting a welcome, or—'

'Me?' Davidh asked. His stepfather had been Iain's natural father's closest friend and had been critical in bringing Iain, and his mother, into the clan. Even finding out her secret—his identity—had not prevented the Cameron commander from marrying her and finding a place for Iain in their clan.

'Aye, you, Davidh.' The chieftain laughed.

'Iain, your mother wanted this for you even when she thought it impossible,' Davidh said. 'May we share this with her?'

'As close as she is to Elizabeth, I suspect she already kens.'

Robert led them out into the hall. Iain half expected the lady to be waiting there for them, for she was integral to the success or failure of everything that happened at Achnacarry Castle, Tor Castle or any other place the clan lived.

Then he remembered the argument and saw, from

the frown that furrowed his brow, that his chieftain remembered it, too.

'But, aye, you may.'

With each step through the hall, Iain found a growing surge of excitement, anticipation, wonder and, aye, pride in succeeding in his quest these last three years. To seek the position to which he was entitled and to become the man who would have made his father proud. Finally, finally it was so close he could almost grasp it. Davidh smacked him on the back as they left the hall and strode down the steps of the keep.

'Come, your mother should hear it from you before the news slips out.'

They found his mother in the stone house outside the walls where she and Davidh lived. On her knees, working in her garden, where she was happiest. And though he suspected her surprise at his news was feigned, her joy was not.

Long ago, when he was a wee lad, the first conversation he remembered having with his mother had been about his father. And, over the years as he grew, it was repeated until the moment when he'd understood that he would never have a place among his father's people.

But through her determination and planning and, aye, even a little plotting and deception, Anna Mackenzie had kept her promise to her son and brought him back to Achnacarry. And she'd found a way to make him a part of the Clan Cameron. Though she was always happy for whatever his path took after that, this elevation, this bond, was the completion of her vow of long ago. One she had risked her own life and happiness to attain for him, in honour of the love she'd shared with his father.

Over the next week as his position as tanist was confirmed and the arrangements for his betrothal that would tie him to the King's family began in earnest, a small niggling thought grew within him, detracting from the complete exhilaration and anticipation he should feel. Oh, his kith and kin offered their good tidings and best wishes. His men, the ones with whom he'd trained and served over these last three years, made certain to celebrate and it was a night he would not easily forget…if he could indeed remember it.

Yet, as he now mounted his horse to ride out to the mill, where some damage needed to be repaired, a small regret yet burned within him. If only…

If only it had happened differently.

If only they'd been ready three years ago.

If only…

Iain shoved such regrets about lost love and missed opportunities from his thoughts as he rode with a small group of workers towards the mill out in the forest. Being tanist was not the lofty thing in the Camerons that it might be in other clans. Here, his chieftain expected his hard and varied labours and experience to continue to build until the time he was needed by his clan. Tearing out trees or putting millstones aright was the exact kind of work he needed right now to clear his thoughts and gather his concentration.

The past would remain in the past, but the future, Davidh would always say, was in your own hands.

Chapter Two

'So, our new tanist is not just beauty, but brawn as well!'

'Leave off, Baen,' Iain said through clenched teeth. 'Grab there.'

Iain's tentative hold on the large stone nearly slipped, which would allow it to slide back to the floor inside the mill-house…again…for the third time since they'd begun trying to reposition it. And for the second since the rains had made everything they tried nigh to impossible.

He could not fault Baen or any of the others for not being able to manage the huge stone. Between its unwieldiness, weight and wetness, it was like trying to get a hold on one of the thrashing fish when taken from the waters of the loch. But it was not any of those obstacles keeping the millstone from working.

'I think ye are right, Iain,' James called out. The miller had been guiding the wooden axle so it was ready to insert into the stone. ''Tis the fit of it that doesna match the hole.' The loud collective groan echoed through the building as the men eased the stone back to the floor. 'The axle pole will need to be carved anew,' James said. The exhaustion and frustration filled his voice and stance. 'That will take days.'

Iain stepped back and wiped his hands together.

'I can help.' Iain had always had a talent for working with wood and his skills had led him to training in carpentry. For years after his arrival in Achnacarry, he'd served the clan using his abilities in that manner.

'Come now, tanist,' Baen said. 'The chieftain expects more of you than cutting down trees.' Sometimes he could abide his friend's teasing, but at times like this it was more a nuisance. Iain shook his head, trying to warn his friend off before he pushed this too far.

'As tanist, 'tis my responsibility to see to the welfare of the clan and its village. Now, see to your task and let me see to mine.' Baen held his hands up and backed away.

'We need to find the tree and prepare it before we can place it. Get Lachlan Dubh to do that—he has the best eye for that kind of thing,' Iain said. He nodded at another of his men, who turned at this order and walked off to see to it. Though one of the millstones would not be working, there were two others that would. 'What do we have to do before the tree is ready, James?'

After James had set out a plan for replacing the wooden axle followed by a repositioning of the millstone, Iain stretched, trying to loosen up. He'd not done this kind of labour in a long time and his body reminded him with tightness and cramping in his arms and back. Rolling his shoulders, he gazed out into the thick growth of trees around the mill and the miller's cottage. A blur of movement further down the stream and the sight of a bit of a bright colour different from the browns and greens of the trees and bushes caught his eye. He could not explain why he knew it was a woman, nor why he would care. But he stared for some time, curious about who it could be.

This was far enough from the village and the keep that it would be unusual for it to be someone who lived there. And James's family had all gone inside their nearby cottage when the rains had begun earlier this morn.

Iain watched until he could no longer see it and turned back to the men. They had several hours of work yet ahead of them even without being able to replace the broken wooden pole.

James's wife, Coira, and their daughter brought them food at midday and his son worked alongside them. Only as the men were gathering their tools and readying to return to their task did he hear the casually made comments between father and son about helping out a visitor, a woman, staying a short distance away from the mill. So there had been someone out in the woods earlier. And his suspicion that it was a woman was correct as well.

Lachlan Dubh arrived later, after the rain had stopped and the skies cleared, and it took the old man little time to choose a tree that would fit their needs. They would let the wood dry a bit before shaving it down, layer by layer, until it was the thickness needed to fit the opening in the millstone.

No matter the task in front of him and his attention to it and those working with or around him, his curiosity about this visitor had tickled his interest. When the others headed back to the village, he walked in the opposite direction, tugging the reins and bringing his horse along with him. Following the course of the stream towards the loch, he searched ahead for any signs of the mysterious visitor.

He'd walked about a good distance when he heard it. A woman crying. Nay, crying was too mild a word for the sound of utter devastation that echoed to him from the shadows off the path. Iain made his way towards it, towards her, taking quiet steps to avoid surprising her. He just wanted to find out the cause of her crying. Why? It made no sense, he just knew that he must.

He approached a small cottage and tied the reins to a tree to keep his horse from bolting. A path led off from it and Iain simply walked, listening to the despair in each sob until he stood a short distance behind her.

From the moment she'd opened her eyes this morn, a nervousness had filled her. It seemed that the longer she was here, resting with few, if any, demands on her time or efforts, the more the emptiness within her ached. And that ache was something new and different…and even the awareness of it was unexpected as well.

Glynnis moved through the small daily chores she'd taken on or that Maggie had somehow managed to give to her. Some time after their midday meal, she noticed that the rains had eased and the sun had won its battle over most of the clouds. Her maid had to encourage her to walk outside each day, especially when her vow to see the mill had not been fulfilled, but this day, a need to go out unfurled within her.

By the time she pulled the door closed behind her, Glynnis had trouble taking a breath. And she began to run. Only reaching the stream stopped her. Falling to her knees, the sobbing began without warning. She leaned over, her face in her hands, and let out the pain that bubbled from deep inside.

The pain took her breath away. She'd believed she was empty of the guilt and the grief and the loss, but they rose up and pushed their way out. The lies. The deaths. The births worse than death. All of it poured from her soul and from the heart she thought was numb. Rocking on her knees, she wrapped her arms around herself and let it all free.

Glynnis never heard his approach until he spoke.

'Mistress? Are you well?'

She sucked in a breath and tugged her shawl tighter around her. Who would be this far from the village?

'Mistress? Do you need help?'

His voice moved slightly closer and now panic filled her. Who was he? Though he did not sound threatening, she did not wish to be seen, especially like this. But also, her invitation from Lady Elizabeth promised her a quiet and isolated place where she could shut herself away from…the world.

'Mistress?'

'I am well,' she whispered without looking over her shoulder. 'I need no assistance.'

Glynnis held her breath, waiting for the man's next action. Would he come closer or leave her be? His identity mattered not. She just wished to be left alone.

'If you are certain?' About to reply, Maggie called out.

'I will assist my...cousin, sir,' her maid said. 'She has been ill.' Maggie reached her side, boldly moving between her and the man. 'Come, Clara.' Without facing the man, Glynnis allowed her maid to guide her back towards the cottage.

'I wish you well, Mistress.'

She'd taken a few steps when something about his voice struck her. Some familiar tone in it reminded her of...someone. Glynnis kept her head turned away and walked at Maggie's side until they reached the door. Stepping inside, she made her way to the other small window near the back of the cottage. Opening one of the shutters, she remained in the shadows as she watched the man who'd tried to help her mount his huge black horse and ride away down the road that would lead to Achnacarry.

Once again, she was struck by a sense that she'd seen him before. He was tall, dark-haired and had the stance and stature of a warrior. From this distance she could not see his face clearly, so it was impossible to tell anything more about him.

'Do ye ken the man, my lady?' Glynnis shook her head as she closed the window and turned from it.

'I ken not, Maggie.' She dropped her shawl away

from her face and shrugged. 'Someone travelling from the mill? Did you not say there was some problem there?' That would make sense.

'Aye, Edward said…something broke inside the mill and men would be working there for several days, if not longer.'

Glynnis watched the man until she could no longer see him through the trees.

It had been three years, three long and trying years, since she'd been here last and she doubted not that she would remember many of the villagers. She'd met many of them during her years here, but people grew older and changed and might have even moved to other properties belonging to the clan. And many others might have…died since she knew them. As many had in her life since her departure from here. But he must have been someone she'd met before.

'Here, my lady, try this.' Maggie held out a cup of steaming liquid to her. 'Lady Elizabeth sent the herbs herself. Said it would calm ye down…or ease yer worries if ye sipped it.'

Glynnis's hands shook as she reached for the cup. She'd learned quickly that her maid's stubbornness ran deep and it would do little good to resist her efforts. Walking to the chair nearer to the hearth, she sat and sipped as commanded. A short time passed in silence as she drank, and enjoyed, the fragrant brew. She knew that the herbs came not from Lady Elizabeth but from her healer, Anna.

Iain's mother.

She'd not thought of him in a long time. If truth were told, she'd forced him and all he stood for from her thoughts. Marriage for love? Following her heart? A man beneath her in position and consequence? He had been all those things when she had I—

Although he'd not been happy when she'd left, but something that had been borne out in time was that she had spared him the disappointment of never having a son of his own if they'd married. Tears burned once more and she pushed the memories of him away as she'd learned to do before.

It mattered not. Lady Elizabeth had assured her, without her even having to ask, that she would not see anyone who could interfere or interrupt her seclusion. Glynnis had no doubt that the lady understood that included Iain Mackenzie Cameron.

Glynnis would not take the chance of encountering anyone. She just could not and would not risk the privacy of this place granted her by Lady Elizabeth.

She would not.

Iain turned back several times, looking back at the cottage he'd not been aware of before. The two women had entered and he saw and heard nothing else. Confusion filled him as he made his way back through the village and gates and to the stables. Not about who the woman was and what ailed her, but why it mattered to him.

Although he'd kept his distance from her, he'd fought the urge to rush to her and ease her pain. Oh, the sound of anguish that poured from her hurt him somehow.

He could blame it on his upbringing by his healer mother and her approach in life to helping people. He could explain it away as always hating to see a woman suffering. But neither of those could explain the way hearing her and seeing her huddled body there tore into his gut like the stab of a *sgian dubh* could.

Well, no matter, for that woman was not in need of him, as her cousin had made clear, and he had other responsibilities to see to. The millstone repairs. Cameron clan documents to read. Davidh had even mentioned a short journey to Tor Castle, their southern holding, and training some new men in Achnacarry to serve in protecting that southern castle after recent reports of outlaws.

A busy life, he thought, lifting the cup to his mouth at supper later that night and emptying it in two mouthfuls. A good life awaited him now after his efforts and his planned service to his clan and King. A satisfying life, filled with a wife and bairns and kith and kin around him. The kind of life his father had expected for himself and not attained. Now, Iain would fulfil his destiny as his father's son.

But that night and every night while he worked at the mill, he dreamed of the woman who would never be part of his future. The one whose loss had spurred the changes that had brought him to the life he was gaining. The woman he could not fight for.

Each night his dreams were filled with Glynnis.

Glynnis dreamed for the first time in…months.

Though she remembered almost nothing of those dreams, she sensed that they were pleasant and unlike the nightmares that had plagued her through her pregnancy and Martainn's death and…the rest. Then they disappeared and neither pleasant nor terror-filled dreams had returned over these three months until now.

And she was sleeping better, waking in the mornings feeling rested and refreshed. Being able to sleep well meant that her exhaustion was lifting as well. Though she feared the return of all the emotions that had been numbed lately, at the least, she felt better able to face that flow and whatever else was coming her way.

'My lady?' Maggie interrupted her reverie. 'The men have ridden past, returning to the village.' This area was so quiet that the sounds made by horses on the road echoed out through the trees.

After that encounter, Glynnis had taken to listening for their passing before going out for any walking. She just did not wish to take the chance of facing those who'd known her when she'd lived here before. Memories of those good times might be the very thing that would break her wide open and let any shred of control dissolve into the wind.

For now, she just wanted to walk.

The winds buffeted her as she approached the edge of the stream and followed its path towards the loch. When they became warmer and the dappled sunlight brought added warmth to her face, Glynnis turned into the breezes and stood listening to… nothing. For the first time since her departure from her well-ordered life and unremarkable marriage to Martainn Campbell and arrival here, the silence did not comfort her. There were questions in the winds and they teased her to pursue them. Tempted her to ask them. To find out more.

But, she reminded herself, the answers and her reactions to them would simply cause her pain. Or trigger those other dangerous feelings that would bring all the regrets and loss back into her soul. Worse than those would be the wants and needs and hopes she dare not examine too closely. The ones she'd believed in for too long after she'd left here.

Glynnis walked all the way to the edge of the loch, taking advantage of the longer days of sunlight and her increasing endurance. Each day she had felt her strength returning bit by bit. No longer satisfied sitting and sewing, she understood the meaning of it— her body was healing from the shocking, painful loss of a sudden and too-soon birth of a bairn. A bairn dead after barely taking its, his, first breath. Another bairn consigned to purgatory. Closing her eyes, she made the sign of the Cross and offered up a prayer for the three wee bairns and for Martainn's soul as well.

At the place where the river joined the loch, she crouched down and scooped up some of the cold, clear water to quench her thirst before heading back to the cottage. The scent of the steaming pot of stew wafting from the open window made her stomach growl as she approached.

Another first for her body—hunger and an appetite had begun to return and she discovered that food tasted better now. Even the simple but filling soups and stews that the miller's wife prepared for them were delicious. Coira's fare was wonderful and she and Maggie would guess at which one would arrive at the cottage for their supper.

Since the woman's son or husband usually brought the food to them, Glynnis had not yet met the one responsible for seeing to their needs. Another accommodation extended to her by her godmother so that she would not have to stay at the keep or in the village and could seek the quiet of this more distant cottage without worry. Mayhap that would be Glynnis's next destination to walk now that she'd reached the loch? Glynnis reached out to lift the latch when she heard it.

The crunching sound made when someone walked on the fallen brush and ground cover among the trees.

The hairs on the back of her neck rose and Glynnis stopped with her hand there on the latch. Needing to turn to see and terrified to at the same time, she stood motionless for long moments, waiting for another sign that someone was close by.

Only the usual sounds floated around her now. No movement other than the winds above her that pushed the tall trees into their usual dance. She lifted the latch and only dared a quick glimpse behind her as she shut the door. Though she could see no one, it did not ease the tightness in her stomach. She was certain someone was out there. Not just passing by, for this cottage was out of the way for those going about their day.

A person did not just happen on this place.

They had to come here. Purposely.

So, someone was out there watching.

Watching her.

Chapter Three

Glynnis MacLachlan was in Achnacarry.

Iain had seen her himself, and from his first glance, he could not believe it was truly her. At the moment he had recognised her, he lost his footing from the shock and he had struggled to stay upright and not fall on his arse. And now, hours later, the surprise of her being here once more had not eased.

As he sat at supper with Robert and the chieftain's closest kin and advisors around the table, their conversations swirled around him. The only thing he could think on was…her.

Yet, this Glynnis was different from the one who'd walked out of his life three years ago. This one curled up in a ball and sobbed out her pain. This one walked haltingly as though every step had to be measured and slow. This one did not smile. Even her voice, when she'd warned him off, was hollow and haunted.

Truly, this one was an empty shell of the woman he'd loved. All the life was gone from her and he was not certain he would have recognised her if he had not studied her from where he stood in the cover of the trees.

What had happened to her? And why was she here at all? What of her husband? She had, according to what he'd heard last, married one of The Campbell's sons and was living in Argyll. Though his own marriage would tie him to the Stewart King, the Campbells were closer still. So, where was he?

Iain had questions, so many questions, but approaching her outright made little sense.

'Iain? Are you well?' He raised his gaze and met his mother's across the table. The healer was never far when Anna Mackenzie was present.

'I am,' he said. He took a mouthful of the ale in his cup and forced a smile for her. 'Just thinking on the problems at the mill.' That was a plausible reason for the repairs had not happened yet due to a series of small mishaps and errors.

'Robert is speaking of your coming marriage,' she whispered, nodding her head towards their chieftain. Iain turned to Robert.

'Lady Elen will visit later in the summer to become acquainted with Iain. If all is well…' Robert paused and smiled at Iain '…the marriage will follow.'

His betrothed was a Welsh cousin of the King who could claim Llewelyn the Great as an ancestor through her mother's line. Though a distant relation, it was an honour to be considered for this match. The cheering and good wishes from all at table felt like the long-awaited triumph it should be for him.

No one he knew had actually met the woman who would be his wife, so he had no idea of her personality or appearance. Neither of those mattered, he reminded himself, in a marriage made for alliances and power. If Lady Elen was coming here, she understood the situation as he did and they would find a way to make it work between them. If they were fortunate, softer feelings might grow between them. It was not what he had wanted in a marriage, but it was part of the life he'd chosen.

The speed at which he was able to push his betrothed from his thoughts and fall back to thinking on the woman in the forest cottage took him by surprise. But, when faced with many tasks, he had the ability to focus on what needed doing before those things that were a certainty.

As his betrothal was.

But the matter that was not was the question about Glynnis's return to Achnacarry. And her condition. Someone knew of her presence. Someone must. Arrangements had been made. Her arrival hidden from most. Glancing around those at table, Iain knew in an instant that this, that Glynnis, had been the topic that brought dissension between the chieftain and his lady wife.

So, Lady Elizabeth had arranged it without Robert's knowledge or permission. She must have only revealed it to him when it was accomplished and thus the argument and continuing distance between the two. But had his own mother known? He took a moment to look at her. Other than the concern always in her gaze, nothing else.

His mother would be of no help. Yet he could not simply approach Lady Elizabeth to ask her. Not with the situation already causing strife. Not with his newly made betrothal.

And not with the condition of the woman he'd beheld there in the forest near the loch. Something had torn her apart. Something had destroyed her soul from the sound of the crying that racked her body.

The last thing he wanted was to add to her suffering. If she had wanted him to know of her presence, she would have told him. Would she not? They had parted not as enemies, but as a dutiful daughter and the man who honoured her.

Drinking from his cup that had been filled by a serving maid, he leaned back in his chair and accepted the inevitable. Until he knew more and understood her reasons for being here, he would do nothing. Because doing the wrong thing could endanger her.

'Will you accompany me to Tor Castle on the morrow, Iain?' Davidh asked.

Iain paused before he answered. He'd like nothing more than to go back and see if she was well. To watch her walk and decide if she was improving with each day or if she worsened. To seek out clues to her presence here, alone but for a companion.

She was not his concern.

The realisation struck him suddenly, but it was the truth. Her presence could not be unknown to the chieftain or his wife, so it was not his to follow or question. No matter how…

'We cannot complete work at the mill for a few more days, so, aye, if I am needed there.'

'I think you will benefit from a break from that

work. Robbie was asking about you the last time I was at the castle,' his stepfather said.

They spoke of the arrangements to travel south for a day or two and Iain left them soon after. Climbing the steps that led up to the battlements, he found himself walking the perimeter and staring at nothing. Though the daylight lasted hours more these days as summer approached, his tasks were complete and he could seek his rest for the early start of their ride south. Yet his body was filled with a restlessness he'd not known before.

Not even those times when he'd stood before Robert and asked for his place in the clan. Not when he'd faced challenge after challenge from learning and training to the standards that the chieftain, his stepfather and even he expected of himself. Not even the night he'd offered Glynnis his heart and his future.

He walked around the walls, letting the winds whip past him as he tried to release her from his thoughts. By the time the guards standing at each corner had nodded at him the fourth time he walked by them, he'd given up the hopeless task. When the sun's light had been conquered by the night, Iain sought his chamber.

It seemed that every time his thoughts were filled with her—memories of their time together, memories of these last empty years apart—his night ended with no sleep. As this one did.

As he rode out of Achnacarry the next morning, he promised himself that when he returned, he would find out the truth about Glynnis.

* * *

The pains began two days after her encounter with the stranger. Well, it was not so much an encounter as an awareness of a man somewhere out in the woods. But after the first time, she felt confused and worried that word of her return here would spread. As Glynnis tried to rise that morning, the deep stabbing spasms that pierced through her and took her breath away reminded her of another kind of pain. One she never thought to feel again.

Wave after wave of queasiness followed and dizziness struck quickly, making it impossible to get up from her pallet. She reached out to take hold of something to regain her balance and found nothing. With her head spinning and her stomach threatening to empty non-existent contents, she fell forward. Only Maggie's quick actions saved her from hitting the floor.

When she opened her eyes, her maid stood over her, staring down with a terror-filled gaze and clutching her hand tightly. Almost tightly enough to distract Glynnis from the next series of spasms that tore through her belly.

'My lady! Are ye ill? What do ye need?' Maggie cried out.

She could not explain or understand the pain and when it struck she could not draw a breath. It felt as though she…she was…labouring to give birth.

Which was simply impossible because she'd done that only months ago. The day her husband died. She could not be in labour. Glynnis held on to Maggie's hand.

'Help me rise, Maggie.'

As her maid tugged her up to sit, Glynnis tried to ease her legs over the side of the pallet. Her stomach roiled with every movement and her eyesight blurred, making her head spin. Her strength seeped away and she fell back to lie on the pallet.

Then the pains began anew.

'My lady, ye need help!' Maggie started to cry and Glynnis had not the ability or will to deny it. 'I will go to Coira.'

Glynnis opened her mouth to tell the lass to go, but all that came out was a moan. Unable to breathe when the pain pierced her, she nodded and watched helplessly as Maggie ran out of the door. She could only pray that help would arrive in time. When she felt the blood gushing between her legs, she suspected it would not.

'My lady?' A voice cut through the darkness. 'My lady. Can ye hear me?'

Maggie. Her maid had returned. Had it been hours that she'd been lying here, her lifeblood pouring from her? How was she yet alive?

'Maggie.'

'My lady, Coira is here. She's sent for help. Ye must hold on.'

Glynnis felt hands touching her face and a cool cloth wiped across her brow. She fought to open her eyes, but her body felt so weak she could not.

More time passed and a commotion around her pulled her from her reverie. She struggled against the pain, trying to resist the moans that exploded from deep within with each new tremor.

'My lady? 'Tis Anna. Do you remember me?'

Anna? The healer from Achnacarry? Iain's mother?

'Can you hear me, my lady?' Soft touches brushed her hair back and the cold cloth stroked her cheeks and forehead. 'Can you tell us what happened?'

'Us?' she whispered. Afraid to open her eyes and worsen the dizziness, she lay as still as possible.

'Aye, my lady. Coira is here and your maid, and I brought Lorna, one of our midwives, to help if needed.'

'I am not carrying a bairn.' She forced out the admission. Even saying the words hurt. She would never carry again. Tears burned in eyes she would not open.

'Coira, you can go back to your tasks now. We will see to the lady,' Anna said. 'Maggie, is it? Could you give us a few moments?' Though quiet in tone, the healer cleared the cottage quickly.

'My thanks, Coira,' Glynnis said before the woman left.

'Well, the symptoms your maid spoke of and the bleeding made us suspect you were.' Anna's tone was kind, one that spoke of experience. She'd always been kind to Glynnis. Even when warning her off the inappropriate feelings developing between Glynnis and her son, she had been kind.

'Are the pains as bad now as when they began?' Anna asked.

'Less often now, but just as painful,' Glynnis said, sliding her hand over her belly.

'First, if we can get a sip of this into you, it should help the dizziness and stomach distress.' Anna slid her hand behind Glynnis's head and the other woman supported her shoulders as she guided or rather lifted her from the cushion to take a wee bit of this potion. It was not as vile as many concoctions made by the healer in The Campbell's household and it went down smoothly. After another sip and a few moments, Anna spoke. 'May Lorna examine you, my lady?' She heard Anna shift away.

'Aye.'

The midwife had the same soft touch as Anna as she poked and prodded Glynnis's body. When the pains came again, this Lorna placed her hand over the lower part of Glynnis's belly and waited as the spasms continued. The midwife exchanged a brief glance with Anna before standing and stepping back.

'Let us get you cleaned up, my lady.' Anna reached down for her hand. 'Try to sit up now?'

Whatever had been in the concoction Anna had given her had eased the dizziness and stomach ills and Glynnis was able to lift first her head and soon to sit up. Though her head felt foggy, moving it did not bring on the terrible distress of moments ago.

It took the two efficient and practised women barely any time at all to change the bedding beneath her as well as the soiled gown and shift. Soon, Glynnis found herself sitting in the chair near the hearth, sipping something warm and soothing that seemed to stave off the worst of the spasms. Once Anna and Lorna returned from giving Maggie the sheets and clothing that needed washing—and having the private conversation about her condition—Glynnis knew they would have questions and, hopefully, some answers for her. Anna pulled the other chair closer and Lorna chose to sit on the stool next to the table. For the moment, Glynnis did not feel as close to death as she'd felt before their arrival.

'My lady,' Anna said, 'when did the bleeding start?'

'I had not noticed it until this morn, when I tried to rise.' She glanced at one woman, then the other. 'The pains were so bad that I did not realise I'd begun bleeding until Maggie left to get help.'

'Are yer cycles always this painful, my lady?' Lorna asked. Glynnis shook her head. The midwife let out a breath and continued on. 'Have ye given birth recently?'

'Aye' was all she could get out before struggling against the tears. Anna's gaze was filled with pity when she met it. Nay, not pity. Understanding.

'When, my lady?' Anna whispered.

'Nigh on three months past.'

'And the bairn?' Lorna asked.

'Born too early. He...' She closed her eyes and could see the wee body, not old enough to breathe yet. 'He died within minutes.' The women made the sign of the Cross and whispered words for the bairn's soul.

'Have you bled since, my lady?' She could not look at them, so she shook her head. Lorna leaned over and touched her hand. 'The first time it returns after a birth can be frightening. Your body has changed and nothing will be what it used to be for some time.'

Her explanation made sense. Though she'd not

been in the confidences of many women who'd borne babies, she suspected it was true. The other two times she'd been pregnant, she'd lost them before she'd laboured to give them life. Her recoveries were different each time.

'I suspect that the pains will plague ye for a few days,' Lorna said. 'Anna's potion will ease them if ye take a bit a few times a day while they're at their worst.'

'And listen to yer body, my lady,' Anna added. 'Though I do not recommend laying about too much. Once the dizziness has eased, try to move a bit. Walk if you can. At least a few times each day.'

'Aye, Anna has the right of it. Moving will let your body rid itself of…well, ye ken,' Lorna said.

Glynnis leaned her head on the high wooden back of the chair and allowed Anna to lift the cup from her grip. The two wordlessly collected their supplies and packed them into the baskets they'd brought. Anna leaned closer and said something she could not hear to Lorna. The midwife nodded to Glynnis before leaving her alone with Anna.

Glynnis could feel the awkwardness between them now as she watched Anna's hesitant steps across the cottage. The healer had changed little since they'd last seen each other—time paid no mind to her if you looked for wrinkles or grey hair. Anna looked as young and fit as before.

'You look well, Anna,' she said, offering an opening for the conversation that would not be avoided. 'How is Davidh? Iain?' It would be ridiculous for her not to ask about him now.

'I have been well, my lady. Davidh still serves The Cameron as commander and Iain is now tanist.'

So many questions swirled about her unasked and the woman who'd left him behind three years before would have given voice to them all. But the woman she was now could not manage to find the strength to be truly curious. He was gone from her life and she from his. Nothing could change that.

'And you, my lady? The last I'd heard you had wed The Campbell's son.'

'Wed then and widowed now.' She heard Anna's soft gasp in reaction to her words. 'And aye, his shocking death brought on my labour and killed our bairn.'

Another gasp echoed between them. The sad and strange part of this was that Glynnis was, mostly, numb when she spoke of it. Oh, there were times that the sorrow bubbled up and out like it had that day by the stream, but she was usually able to push it down and not feel the pain of it.

'I am so sorry, Glynnis,' Anna said softly. 'I understand... I am sorry.'

Glynnis stared at the low, flickering flames in the hearth and gave a weak smile, acknowledging the sympathy offered. Anna had suffered loss in her life, too, so Glynnis felt the honesty in her words. She knew the loss of a bairn. And she seemed to understand that Glynnis could not bear more sympathy right in this moment.

'If you agree, Lorna will come to visit you in a day or two. I left the tincture in that bottle.' Anna pointed to the small, stoppered container on the table as she spoke. 'Lorna will bring you more clean cloths and such. If you have need of anything before she comes, send word to me in the village.'

'My thanks, Anna. And to Lorna as well.'

Anna lifted the latch and faced her before leaving. 'This is what brought you back? These losses?' Glynnis nodded. 'I hope you are well soon.'

Glynnis remained sitting, allowing whatever was in that concoction to ease her pain. The spasms seemed to lessen with each passing moment. Her cycle had given no sign of returning after the birth or since until it happened this morn. And she accepted it for what it was now—another sign confirming her failure as a woman, a wife and a mother.

She closed her eyes and tried to stop anticipating the next wave of pain to come. The warmth of the hearth and the comfort of whatever Anna had put in her tea helped in that and soon, the calm and quiet drew her to sleep. Only one clear thought passed through her as she fell.

Iain was tanist of the Clan Cameron.

Chapter Four

Glynnis had found the first one next to the stream where she liked to stand and listen to the calming sounds of the water passing her by. A small, sheltered place with an opening that led to the edge of the water. She found herself there on each walk she took.

Two days later, one sat on the ground, tucked into the roots of the tree next to the spot where Maggie always placed her chair so she could rest if tired from the walking.

And two days after that one, the new one sat boldly in front of her door, just waiting for her to find it. It somehow had been placed there after her maid had left on an errand.

Small, carved wooden animals left for her to find. Even now, her hand traced over the one she'd had the longest—the horse Iain had pressed into her hand as they parted. Three years ago and for that first year without him, she'd rubbed her fingers over it until some of it had worn away. It still served as a worry stone for her.

Now, a cow, a sheep and this dog joined her collection as Iain let her know that he knew of her presence here.

Glynnis suspected he was the man who'd found her sobbing that morning and the one whose nearness had triggered an awareness of being watched. Now, it was just a matter of time before he appeared there instead of his creations.

It had taken only a few days after feeling better for her curiosity to rise. Anna had said he was now tanist to Robert. Yet when they'd parted he was a man skilled in woodworking with some training to fight. A man who was willing to serve his natural father's distant relative who sat on the high seat of the clan.

Though the custom of primogeniture was moving into the clans, many of them, most of the Highland ones that she knew, clung to the old practice of tanistry—choosing a man of the blood who was worthy and strong enough to lead.

And now that was Iain.

Clearly the last three years had wrought changes in both of them—him for the better while her for the worse.

After placing the new addition on the stool by the door, she stood watching and clutching the wooden horse in her hand. She saw movement in the trees nearest the cottage and held her breath as he stepped out of the shadows and into the light. He nodded at her and waited for her to return the acknowledgement. When she did so, he took the first step towards her.

Oh, the changes that the three years had wrought in him!

If her sight and memory were correct, he'd added several inches of height and muscle to his frame since she'd seen him last. His hair was longer now and worn pulled away from his face to expose the strong chin and jawline of a man. His movements were assured and he moved with the grace of a predator stalking his prey. Very different from the lanky gait of the lad on the edge of manhood she remembered. It took only a few long strides to reach her.

A long moment passed as they stood in silence, just looking at each other. For all that she would have sworn she knew him well, the one she knew was another Iain and not this man standing before her. Not this warrior. Not this…tanist.

But neither was she the younger, innocent, hopeful young woman of three years before. What did he see when he looked at her? Did he see beyond the plain gown and single braid? Or had he expected to see her in the finery of her station? Did he see the changes in her body from three pregnancies? Did he see the emptiness within her, not just of body, but of soul and heart?

'Glynnis.' Though he said her name in a near whisper, it was much deeper and more masculine than the last time they spoke. She felt the sound of it pierce through her. It was the first sensation she'd felt that she welcomed in months. 'How do you fare?'

'I am—' She stopped, uncertain of what to say. Had his mother told him what had happened?

Iain reached out as though to take her hand and

paused, as though he knew not whether to touch her. The worst part of that gesture was she did not know if she welcomed his touch or not. After a few moments, he dropped his arm to his side.

'And, nay, my mother did not betray your confidence if that worries you,' he said. 'I had seen you here weeks ago. When she rode out of the village in her wagon without a word or glance, I kenned someone needed her help.' A shrug lifted his shoulders and one corner of his mouth curved into a tentative smile. 'I followed her here and waited for her to leave.'

'She told you nothing?' Glynnis watched his face, trying to acquaint herself with this newer, more masculine, taller version of the Iain she remembered.

'My mother does not say anything she does not wish to share,' he muttered. His tone revealed his lack of success in getting the answers he wanted. 'When I admitted that I kenned you were here, she would only say that you were in no danger.' He shook his head. 'She has not changed from your time here, Glynnis.'

He did step closer and studied her face, staring into her eyes. Glynnis could hardly keep her gaze on his for the intensity made her…feel.

'You have been watching me?'

'Aye, I have been.' This time when he reached for her hand, he took hold of it, encircling it with his much larger one. 'Not truly watching you, just checking on you from time to time,' he admitted. 'When I heard you…' He paused and swallowed hard against whatever he was going to say. 'When I saw you that day, I was not certain it was even you. You have changed.'

Glynnis looked away and tried to keep all the ways

she had changed from her thoughts. None of them good. Many of them bad. A few were terrible.

'Aye,' she whispered as the tears spilled on to her cheeks. His thumb rubbed against her palm in a soothing movement—one she wanted to continue. The sigh escaped her before she could stop it. Lifting her other hand, the one in which she held the wooden horse he'd carved, she rubbed the tears off her cheek with the back of it as best she could.

'Do not greet, Glynnis. I mean you no harm,' he whispered, his thumb never stopping. 'I did not seek you out to cause you such worry.'

Slowly, he released her hand and stepped away. She expected to feel the separation between them. To be aware his touch was gone and that it mattered. But she simply could not feel it. She was so empty.

'Send word to me if you have need of anything,' he said. A smile and a nod followed before he spoke again. 'Though I suspect that Lady Elizabeth is seeing to your comfort and care.' He began walking away and she noticed all the changes in him once more. He turned back to face her. 'Have you heard that the mill requires more work than was first thought?'

At her shrug, he said, 'I will be in this area as long as the work continues.' Ah, his skills in woodworking would come in handy at the mill. That explained his presence in the area. Now he paused as though uncertain he should say whatever he was considering.

'Is aught wrong?' she asked.

'Nay. 'Tis just that I would… If you have… I ken you…' He stopped and shook his head. 'I would like to come and speak with you.'

Confused over his hesitation and the confusion in his gaze, Glynnis touched his hand again. 'What do you mean?'

'I am going to come by to see how you fare.'

He searched her face and she knew he was waiting for her to object or approve. But his words had not asked her. This was a man accustomed to giving orders. A man accustomed to being obeyed. Would he accept her refusal if she raised it?

'Aye.' The word slipped out and seemed to surprise them both.

'Good.' He turned away and walked back towards the path leading to the road without another word.

Once more she was struck by his appearance, both his height and the long, bold masculine strides which covered the distance quickly. He was taller now than Martainn. He did not carry the same weight that her husband had, but Iain's frame appeared just as muscular. Soon, he disappeared and Glynnis stood for a short while longer as questions and curiosity teased the edge of her thoughts.

It felt so strange to want to know more. To feel a niggling there deep in her thoughts about the man he'd become. Glynnis was still in the same position when Maggie returned from visiting Coira. Later, as the soreness in her body continued to ease, those questions began to grow.

For the first time in such a long time, she wondered.

By the time he reached the road and his horse, Iain's frustration and anger showed in his stomping strides. Every foul word rattled around in his head and he tugged the reins free of the branch where he'd tied them. Leading the horse out of the trees, he clutched hold of the saddle and boosted himself on to the strong back of the animal. Urging the horse into a gallop, Iain guided the beast in the opposite direction and followed a different path that took him around the cottage to the loch.

Riding along the shore, he let the horse have his head as the image of Glynnis settled in his thoughts. He'd not seen her face the day he'd found her sobbing in the forest and even knowing that the woman in the cottage was indeed that same one had not prepared him for seeing her just a few feet from him.

Or readied him for the way she looked.

Or for the sorrow that poured from her with every glance and even in the way she held herself as she stood before him.

One thing she did not show was surprise when he stepped out of the cover of the bushes into her view.

Something in the words his mother had spoken had warned him about Glynnis's decline and condition. Oh, his mother would never share private details with anyone, but her tone when she finally admitted the lady's presence spoke all the words she would not. So, seeing Glynnis's eyes bereft and absent of their usual light and sparkle, noticing her body now thinner and fragile and even watching as she struggled to speak to him tore into him like a dull dagger.

Iain pulled on the reins and his horse drew to a stop as he slid off. Wrapping the reins around his fist, he led the animal to the edge so he could drink.

Why had he gone to the cottage? Iain stared across

the calm surface of the loch. Knowing that the occu-
pant was indeed the one woman he should not seek
out had not stopped him. There were many excuses
he could make about why he'd followed her or why
he'd watched her, but at the heart of it, Iain needed to
see her. He needed to speak to her. He needed to discover if her decision to leave him behind three years
ago had benefitted her as it had him.

He scooped up several stones and pitched them one
at a time across the surface of the water, watching as
they skipped and dropped into the loch's depths. So
many questions filled his thoughts, but it took only
a brief glimpse of the broken, suffering woman to
scatter them like leaves in the wind.

She had always been the most patient, the most
kind, the most generous and the most sensitive person he'd known. He'd spent most of his early years
as the son of the healer living in the village of his
mother's kin. Glynnis had been the first noblewoman he'd spent time around and she'd treated
him as though he mattered. Though she'd come to
Achnacarry as the woman his cousin would likely
marry, it had not taken long for him to fall in…

Whatever had happened to her these last years had
turned her into an empty husk of that lovely, kind
young woman. And no one, especially not Glynnis,
deserved to suffer so. What could have caused this
change? He'd spied no signs of a husband with heavy
fists, though those signs could be hidden. No injuries were apparent. But they were sometimes not in
view either.

After thinking about the changes in her, Iain understood that those were not the only matters that bothered him.

Though he'd felt aggrieved to know she'd returned weeks ago and kept her presence here a secret, in truth he'd never once asked after her once she'd left. He'd purged her from his thoughts and his heart with weeks of overindulging in hard spirits. Accepting her refusal and departure for a separate future had been the impetus for the changes in him.

Yet thinking on that now, he wondered why he'd never asked after her once in the years since she'd gone. Had it been pride that held him back? Fear? Loathing for the weakness she was to him? He was certain that Lady Elizabeth or even Sheena, Robbie's wife, would have kept in touch with her, even if they never mentioned her to him after his reaction to her leaving.

Then, after those first weeks, he'd plunged into chasing his dream of taking his rightful place, as his father would have.

So, why now?

Why did he care?

He was accomplished now, on the brink of a betrothal that would not have been possible just a short time ago, and already accepted as the man who would take the high chair next. He could stand on his feet and face most every one of the chieftain's warriors now. He could read and write.

So, why did a woman from his past matter to him? A woman who had no place in his life.

And why did the urge, nay, the need to speak with her grow with every breath he took? Even now, his thoughts were turning to how to accomplish that—speaking to her alone—even while carrying out his duties. Even while knowing he could not do this openly. But see her he would.

His decision made, Iain walked back, untangled the reins and mounted his horse. He would be missed if he did not return for the evening meal at the keep—something expected of him by Robert. More than that, his mother would be waiting for his explanation. With each passing day, she'd taken note of his old habit as had his stepfather who showed their concern with a raised brow or an unguarded frown when they witnessed him carving another piece of wood.

An unexpected visitor at the keep allowed him to avoid more scrutiny. Iain took his customary seat at the table, one nearer to one end than the middle, and welcomed Robbie Cameron's arrival.

'I did not expect to see you here, Rob,' Iain said, as the servant filled the bowl before him with a thick stew. Their meals were plain but filling, as the chieftain liked unless there were guests who needed to be impressed with finer fare. 'Is Sheena with you?' He looked around the table for any sign of his cousin's wife.

'Nay,' Rob said. 'She did not feel up to travelling, so she remained behind.' The happy tone in his words did not match his report of Sheena's possible illness. And that was the clue that Iain finally understood and he smiled back.

'Truly?'

'Aye,' Rob said, glancing at those close enough to

hear their conversation. 'Though none but my father and mother ken yet.' Sheena was carrying. From Rob's daft grin, he was immensely pleased by her condition.

'I am pleased for you both,' Iain said.

'The midwife said the worst of it should pass soon, which will please Sheena.' Rob lowered his voice to almost a whisper. 'But for the time being…' Rob puffed out his cheeks and took on the look of someone whose belly was threatening to empty.

At Rob's words, a memory flickered in Iain's thoughts. He'd seen not only his mother leaving the cottage where Glynnis was, but also the village woman who helped with…births.

Lorna.

The midwife had tended to Glynnis.

'Aye, that's the expression Sheena has been wearing for weeks now, Iain. A bit greenish. A bit worried and a bit more surprised by it all.'

'I hope all goes well,' he said. Drinking down the ale in his cup, he let the topic drop.

As supper progressed, he thought on little else but Glynnis and the meaning of the midwife's visit to her. Strange if she was here and her Campbell husband remained behind. And if the man had travelled with her, notice would have been taken, for the man's presence here would be uncomfortable at best. Though allies to the Mackintoshes, the Camerons and the Campbells were not on good terms. The chieftain's son would need their chieftain's permission to be here. And if Robert had granted such approval, Iain would have been informed.

He had so many questions and no one who could

answer them—save one. The one he would not take the chance of asking. Not with her haunted eyes and gaunt face and fragile bearing. Iain would have to take his time to learn her secrets or at least uncover her reasons for being here.

'Are you too high in the chieftain's regard that you no longer stand guard?'

Robbie laughed as Iain made a gesture to answer the insult given. Serving as a guard, walking the walls and checking the gates and outbuildings was one of the first duties Iain was assigned to when he'd asked for a chance to serve. Achnacarry, being the main estate of The Cameron, was both highly protected and well secured. Every able man served as a guard at some time in his life. Robert believed that no one was too high or low to protect the clan.

'Come and see if you remember how 'tis done,' Iain said as he stood and waited on Robert to give him leave with a nod of his head.

They reached the top of the keep and walked to the far corner before speaking, a practice they'd begun when one of them needed the counsel of a friend. And, over the years they'd grown up together, it had happened many times. After a short time, and as the guards took up new positions away from them, Iain broke the silence.

'So, when is this new Cameron expected?'

'God willing, midwinter.'

'Will you stay at Tor or bring her here for the birth?'

Robbie shrugged. 'We will wait to see her through the next months and decide that.'

Bearing a child was the most dangerous thing a woman could do, even though it was the one thing expected in marriages made for heirs.

Iain stared across the yard and listened as the sounds of the day faded even as the light remained strong. The nights grew shorter as summer was upon them. In winter, it would be fully dark before they ate their evening meal. But now, it would be light enough to ride by for several more hours.

Robbie cleared his throat and let out a loud breath, gaining Iain's attention. Which had been his friend's purpose after all.

'Is it the betrothal that vexes you?' Robbie asked. Iain met his friend's intense stare. 'Or being named tanist so quickly?'

'Neither of those,' he said. He spoke the truth, for he'd not spent a moment worrying over either of those two matters. 'Something else.'

'Some*one* else?' Robbie's gaze narrowed. Iain nodded.

'Did Sheena continue to write to…Glynnis when she left?' he asked.

'She did.' Robbie was going to make this difficult.

'Even after she married?'

'Aye.'

Iain faced his cousin and shoved his shoulder. Robbie's laughter told Iain he was right—the man was being a pain in the arse on purpose. So, Iain shoved him again, slamming him up against the wall.

'Hold!' Robbie laughed once more as he held up his hands in surrender. He tugged his tunic and plaid back into place and nodded. 'Aye. Sheena has written and heard from Glynnis since she married. She heard from her every few months until…a short time ago.' Robbie crossed his arms over his chest and studied him. 'Why do you ask this? And why now?'

Was it wise to tell him all of it? If the only risk was speaking to his father about it, well, Iain knew that their chieftain was aware of and not happy about the lady's presence here. The disagreement between the laird and his wife made sense when his own mother had made him swear not to reveal what he knew. When he did not reply, Robbie smiled.

'I think the betrothal has you more worried than you would like.'

Iain backed up and turned away, taking a stance against the wall and looking over the yard once more. Let Robbie think what he might, if it would get Iain what he wanted—more information about what had happened to Glynnis.

'Mayhap.'

'You must ken that I am not the man to give advice about arranged marriages,' Robbie said. 'But, considering how mine turned out, I can recommend it to you.'

Robbie and Sheena had been betrothed when they believed they hated each other. Only a fool, as Robbie had been for some time, could not see the truth, and the love, there between them. It had taken serious strife and a huge risk on Robbie's part for them to find their way.

'You kenned Sheena, mayhap too well, but you had knowledge of each other. With the King's cousin, 'tis different.'

'Well, my friend, what would make you not marry the King's Welsh relative? Looks? Demeanour?' Robbie reached out and tapped Iain's shoulder. 'In truth you ken none of that will stop this from happening.'

Iain had not been concerned with the betrothal. He brought it up only to steer Robbie's questions away from his interest in Glynnis, but now he suspected he should be. He glanced at Robbie's face and understood the truth in his words.

'There is nothing that will stop it,' he admitted.

'Just so,' Robbie said, smacking Iain's shoulder. 'And the benefits of this marriage—for you, our clan and even the King and lady herself will smooth out any roughness in the road to it.'

Accepting his cousin's words, Iain nodded and turned to leave. He'd almost reached the place where the guards on duty had retreated when Robbie spoke again.

'Was there anything in particular about Glynnis you wanted to ken?'

Chapter Five

Days had passed and Glynnis felt stronger with each
one.

And, for the first time, a small amount of disappointment filled her as another day passed without
Iain's promised return. After that, an unexpected niggling of curiosity happened when Maggie mentioned
some inconsequential comment the miller had made
about Iain's skills in carving and finishing all manner of wood structures. What was his life like now as
tanist? When had that happened? Her gaze even now
returned to her bed, where she'd placed the growing
menagerie of animals carefully under the pallet and
out of sight.

For months, she'd simply reacted and never looked
more closely at the people, places or situations around
her. Feeling anything after losing so much hurt too
unbearably so she chose to push it all away instead.
Her body and heart could not heal with such grief inside her. With this new interest to know more about
him came the realisation that mayhap she was ready

to begin healing. Mayhap she could live once more. Mayhap the emptiness in her heart would ease and she would find something that made her smile?

The days passed in much the same way as the ones before—waking, breaking her fast, mending or sewing, taking a walk in the forest, sometimes napping when her strength gave out, supping and seeking her rest at night. Maggie had guided her those first weeks, but now the slow pace of her life chafed a bit. Though a lady by birth and marriage, she had always been busy. Tasks to complete, chores to do or to oversee, and more filled her days.

Marriage had changed some of that, pregnancy others, but hours of leisure were something she was not accustomed to at all. At least not for long. She had lingered in her sickbed after losing the first two bairns, that had been early in each of those pregnancies and the bodily changes were quickly gone. So life went on after those losses.

The loss this time had defeated her. When Martainn's shocking accident and death brought on her labour, the bairn had struggled for life even as she fought to live. The boy, the heir Martainn craved so much, passed and Glynnis gave up.

She let go of life, too. She let go of being concerned about…anything around her. Only Martainn's mother, consulting with Glynnis's godmother, saved her life by arranging this stay.

But now, now a small shift was beginning within her. Her body was healing from the physical loss. Her strength was rebuilding within her. And these last few days, emotions were rising and she recognised them.

The soft knock on the door startled her from her reverie. She had not stopped sewing the rend in the tunic even as her thoughts swirled, but now she placed it down and watched as Maggie opened the door. His now deeper voice was soft as he spoke.

'I have come to speak with the lady,' he said. Maggie tugged the door open wider and Glynnis nodded when he saw her there.

'I am here.' Glynnis stood and smoothed her gown.

'Will you walk? The night is pleasant and there are a few hours of sunlight left.'

Glynnis noticed Maggie's interested gaze as she looked back and forth between the two of them. Now she stared at Glynnis, awaiting her answer to this invitation. The girl knew who Iain was, even if she did not know the story of their past. Few here knew the whole of it and those who did would not gossip about it.

Glynnis nodded and walked to the door. As she stepped outside, Maggie handed her a shawl. Iain moved back to allow her to pass him. Uncertain of where to go, Glynnis waited for him. Iain stepped to her side and walked in the direction of the path she usually took.

He had watched her over the last weeks.

At first his strides were longer and faster than hers, but in little time he adjusted his gait to remain by her side. They had walked out like this a number of times when she'd lived here before and it felt familiar and soothing. Truly, the only bad part of loving Iain had been the leaving.

She stumbled at that thought and he caught her

arm, holding her elbow until she steadied. She noticed he did not relinquish his hold immediately, but used it to guide her down the path that led to the loch. They walked in silence for a short distance and he dropped his arm to his side.

'So, do you plan to visit the village during your stay?' he asked as they reached the turn in the path. He slowed his pace.

A polite enquiry on his part, but being asked as a question, and the expectation of a reply startled her. Her husband's family simply left her on her own during the days and weeks after his death—she was consulted about nothing. Not his funeral and burial. Not their bairn's.

'I think not,' she said as they continued on.

'There are many who would enjoy seeing you. Many remember you fondly from your time here.'

'I fear 'tis not as simple as walking into the village, Iain. 'Tis…complicated.'

Without facing her, he made a little sound that was like a huff while not quite. A memory of that sound echoed in her thoughts, but she could not bring it clearly to mind. The sound was a familiar one. A habit he'd had when presented with something unexpected. Glynnis waited for him to challenge her words or to invite her to say more. When she did not, he made that little sound and continued on.

'Are you well, Glynnis? With my mother's attendance, and Lorna's, I suspect that your health is—'

'Improving,' she said before he could say more. His question would lead to another and another and more along a path she did not wish to tread. 'I am better with each passing day.'

Whether due to their pace or the tension and fear that ran like the stream's current within her, Glynnis found herself short of breath. Pausing before her control of the panic grew unmanageable, she forced herself to breathe more slowly. He surprised her by holding out his flask to her.

'A wee sip of this will ease your worries, Glynnis.' She just stared at the offering, undecided about accepting or rejecting it. The expectant glimmer in his gaze convinced her.

He tugged it open and held it up to her mouth. She drew a small taste of it and let it slide over her tongue and down her throat. The burn almost overwhelmed her, but she did not fight the potent brew as it slid down into her stomach. She swallowed once more and the warmth spread out from her belly and into her limbs. When his arm slipped around her waist, she allowed it.

They walked along, reaching the place where she stopped by habit, and he guided her to the edge of the water. The sun dipped down behind the hills in the distance, adding a chill to the summer evening. Whether from the heat of his body so close to hers or the feeling of the spirits spreading through her blood, Glynnis only knew she did not shiver as was usual for her lately if not near a blazing hearth.

'Is there something here that draws your attention, Glynnis? I notice you stop in this place often.'

His voice, closer than she'd realised it, teased her

with its softness. The revelation of his watching her forced a question.

'How many times have you watched me walk?'

A pause suggested he would not answer her question. He let out a breath.

'Too many.' His shrug rubbed against her shoulder. 'Curiosity drew me here at first. As tanist, I need to be aware of everything that happens here in Achnacarry and in the clan.' He faced her without moving his arm from its place around her. 'Then, when I realised you were…ill and my mother would give me no information about you, I began watching and waiting for you to leave the cottage. To see if you were yet in need of help. To see if you were well.'

'Iain.' Uncertain of what else to say, she glanced away.

'I thought we parted as friends, Glynnis. How could I ignore a friend in need?'

Why had he said that? In the time since their parting, Glynnis had pushed all memories of him, of them, from her mind and even now she could not bring them back. She would not. Danger lay in doing that. In looking at what could have been. At what had been.

So, what was left between them besides the memories she refused to dredge up? Glynnis drew on years of training in the behaviour expected of a woman of noble birth and allowed the habits of those years to curve her mouth into a practised smile.

'Aye, Iain. I would not expect you to do that. I appreciate that you sought out the truth,' she said.

She hoped she'd imbued the words with more confidence than she felt. When he smiled back, she nearly lost her breath at the unadulterated male beauty that met her gaze. Gone was the boyish expression and in its place were the rugged angles of a man's face. It had been a long time since the smile of a man had caused her mind to muddle, but in this moment, she could not think of a thing to say.

'The warmth and light are fading,' he said, pulling her out of her confusion. 'We should head back to the cottage before you take a chill.'

When he took her by the hand, she allowed it, surprised at the little waves of…feelings that raced through her. His touch. His nearness. His breath near her ear. His voice. All things she'd not taken notice of for a long time.

Their walk back took little time, for they'd not made it very far from the cottage, and soon she saw Maggie standing in the open doorway watching them. He released her hand and she continued alone to the waiting servant, who stepped back to allow her entrance. Glynnis looked back to say…something…to him, but Iain had already turned towards his horse tied to the tree nearest the cottage.

In her enthusiasm, Maggie nearly pushed Glynnis inside and had her sitting next to the hearth, wrapped in a shawl and sipping a cup of Anna's herbal concoction before the sound of his departure dissipated. Though her servant gave her a number of expectant glances, Glynnis was not tempted to speak about Iain or his appearance here.

'Twas simply a meeting of two long-separated friends.

A chance to remember a more pleasant time in her life.

If she could allow the memories free.

If she dared.

Exhaustion filled her as she finished the tea and she allowed Maggie to help her ready for bed. Her body welcomed sleep while her thoughts did not. For the first time in months, curiosity crept in and a single question tasked her mind.

When would he return?

As it turned out, the answer to that question was two days later.

Though the sight of this new Iain, sitting astride his horse outside her door and staring at her with an intensity and confidence that made her shiver, surprised her, she was not unhappy about his arrival. A twinge of pleasure made her smile as he spoke her name.

'Would you ride with me?'

Glynnis glanced around and saw only one horse— his. Did he mean that she should…? His outstretched hand was the answer. It would not be the first time she'd ridden with him. A fleeting memory of a sunny day and the long path alongside Loch Lochy on the way to Tor. The wind lifting her hair and their laughter echoing out behind them as they raced south.

A carefree time.

Before…

'What were you thinking on just now? You smiled at some thought.' He yet held out his hand, waiting for her to take it.

'A memory of another day and another ride,' she admitted. That truth and accepting it startled her.

''Twas not uncommon for us,' he said. 'Until…'

She reached out for his hand, not making the decision to do so, but doing it anyway. 'Until?'

His smile was a sad one as he pulled her up and guided her across his legs. 'Until we had to leave it behind for the responsibilities that awaited us.'

Glynnis chose not to reply to that mild way of describing what had happened between them. As he wrapped his arms around her and adjusted his hold on the reins, she waited for him to urge his horse forward. Although the specific memories were vague in her recollection, her body's response was quite clear—she leaned back into his embrace as though that ride had been just yesterday and not more than three years ago.

For a moment, she was the carefree younger woman who used to ride with him. One whose proper behaviour slipped a bit around Iain Mackenzie. He had been her weakness. Her guilty transgression. Her…past.

Glynnis straightened away from him, holding herself upright even in his embrace. He eased his hold to accommodate her, now touching his heels to the horse's sides and clicking his tongue. This time, he kept the horse to an even pace, not galloping as they had before.

Glynnis closed her eyes and enjoyed the ride. Though she should be worried about being seen with him and even being with him, she took this as a gift. The warmth of the sun on her uplifted face made her smile.

When they broke through the line of trees and reached the river, he turned them towards Loch Arkaig and pressed his knees to the horse's sides to gain speed. They reached a full gallop quickly. She did lean back against his chest, telling herself it was about not interfering with his control of a running horse. She'd be foolish to do anything that could.

'I have ye,' he whispered in her ear. His arm shifted, lying across her stomach just beneath her breasts. 'Just a bit further now.'

Her body felt alive in his arms. For weeks and weeks, months now, she'd forced herself to rise each day and sleep each night. After sitting unmoving, uninvolved, in life for so long, it was as if she had awakened from a deep slumber and was readying for…something.

Glynnis held on to the horse's mane and looked ahead to see where he took her. This was not familiar to her. It was too far for her to walk here and she'd never even tried it before. Iain guided the horse along a different path, one that led away from the loch. They slowed and stopped and Iain jumped down from behind her and reached up to help her.

She walked at his side into the woods and soon they reached a small shelter. It was little more than a shieling which was built in the far reaches of the grazing lands and used when men were caught out there while tending or gathering the cattle or sheep. This was about half the size of the cottage in which she was staying. But this structure, though simple, appeared newer than the one where she resided.

'Come inside,' Iain said as he lifted the latch,

pushed open the door and stood back for her to enter first.

With no expectations about this place, Glynnis was surprised that curiosity about what and why grew within her. She walked to the centre of the shelter and turned around, taking it all in as he lit several lanterns. With no windows to let the sunlight in and even with the door left ajar a bit, the space was too drenched in shadows to examine well. The lanterns caught flame and Glynnis lost her breath at what she saw around her.

Chapter Six

There it was.

Finally.

A spark that told him he was not wrong.

A hint that the woman he'd known did still exist within the shell of the one who'd arrived here all those weeks ago. From her previous lack of response, he'd thought she would refuse his offer. But he'd taken care to move and approach her in a slow but consistent manner, trying to ease her back into being comfortable in his presence.

When Sheena MacLerie first arrived in Achnacarry, she'd referred to Glynnis as 'Lady Paragon MacVirtue' within his hearing. It was not in a mocking way—in truth, it was more of a compliment meant, for she'd tried to capture the way Glynnis was, to describe who she was. Trained to be ever gracious, always polite and never less than a lady, Glynnis treated those around her as was expected of the perfect noblewoman who had all the attributes needed to marry the nobleman who would be her husband.

She could oversee a household and the servants, read and write, keep an accounting, embroider, sew, and her needlework was efficient and lovely. Lady Elizabeth praised her gracefulness and modesty. Sheena learned from her. Everyone held her in the highest regard.

The only time she allowed herself to behave outside the narrow path on which she lived was with him. Glances filled with longing. A few stolen kisses. But what he remembered most was holding her close in those precious encounters he managed to arrange for them.

And, when she allowed herself to relax in his arms while riding here, all of the memories, all his hopes and dreams, awakened even as his need for her did.

Iain watched as she turned in a circle, seeing the place he called his own. He'd begun this as an escape, when the challenge he'd set for himself grew unbearable. Oh, he'd been bold and proud and certain he could do what he must to take his place, but when the true depth and breadth of the changes he faced became clear, his resolve nearly broke.

She walked a few paces to the workbench he'd built first.

Lachlan Dubh, the man who had guided him as he learned, refined and strengthened his woodworking skills, had gifted Iain with his own tools when the old man's hands could no longer hold them. Iain had brought them here and continued to use them and his abilities to find a refuge from the onslaught of demands.

His gaze lingered on the way her hands moved

over the table, following the scars carved into its surface from hours of work. Her finger traced the outline
of the piece of wood he'd left there the last time he'd
been here. She palmed the yet-unformed bit while
staring at the other chunks of wood and the fragments
already chipped away around it.

The form was not yet defined though it was based
on a fish he'd caught in the loch years ago. With a
few hours of carving and smoothing and cutting the
correct angles and curves, the scales would appear.
The head with its gaping mouth would gain definition and the tail would take shape. For now, it was a
rough-cut form of what it would become.

Much as he'd been when he'd sought out the peace
of this shelter. Something wrought of his own hands,
with his well-honed skills. Skills he knew and understood and felt to the marrow of his bones. Skills no
one could question or undermine.

'When did you build this?'

Her words came out on a soft breath. She blinked
several times as though it had surprised her, but she
had not actually asked a single question since they'd
encountered each other so it was something different.

He glanced around the simple structure and
smiled, trying to remember the exact moment when
he'd made the decision. It had not been at the time
she'd left or even in the first weeks or months after
it. Then, he remembered.

'About…' he started to say, but he paused. 'Just
over two years.' He walked to her side and picked
up the chisel. 'I needed a place where no one could
find me.'

She met his eyes and there was something there he'd not seen recently. Interest. Her recent empty gaze, the one that drew him closer and made him want to be near her, was different now. A spark of curiosity was there in those dark brown eyes.

Finally.

'You are the tanist now?'

Another question. Iain wanted to shout for joy at it, but he tempered that reaction and nodded. Lifting the piece of wood from her hand, he turned it over, and noticing the warmth from her grasp, he placed the chisel on it. A few chips and he spoke.

'I am,' he said, keeping his gaze on the chunk of wood in his hand. 'The chieftain and elders confirmed me just months ago.'

'I am...' He heard the breath she pulled in and released. Another stroke over the surface of the wood. 'I am confused over how it came about, Iain. Should Tomas not be?'

He thought on her words and how to answer. Her hand placed on his arm stopped him.

'I mean no insult by my question. I simply thought that with the way of things, 'twould fall to Tomas.' The warmth of her touch disappeared. He'd noticed.

'It would have, but I wanted it.' His hand pushed with a bit too much force and the chisel slid off and skittered across the surface of the worktable.

'I am glad you were chosen,' she said.

He felt her move away and he watched at the edge of his gaze as she explored the rest of his refuge. The need to explain it all burned within him, but he understood that it was not the time to speak of it. Whatever had happened to her, whatever reason brought her here, the damage was apparent. She was in no way able to carry the weight or the truth of his decision on her shoulders. Not now. Not this hollowed-out soul.

'There is wine in the skin there.' He pointed to it. 'If you are thirsty.'

Somehow, he understood she could not withstand the questions he wanted to ask her about her situation. Her unmentioned marriage. Her purpose here other than some kind of respite. So, he kept his attention on the carving in his hand while she did indeed seek out the wine.

Iain followed her progress around the small chamber, noticing each time she stopped and examined something for a moment longer than another. Three things drew her notice—a sketch tacked to the wall, another partially carved block of wood and a finished one. Out of the corner of his eyes he saw her hand lift towards that one, but she dropped it before touching the piece.

Dear God, what had brought this change to her? What had broken her so? Though not part of his life any more, the urge to help her, to fix her, bubbled up from within him. Surely it would be a sin to ignore such pain?

'How often do you come here?'

Her soft question surprised him again. And it revealed to him the biggest change in her behaviour, in her, since they'd last met. Glynnis MacLachlan had never hesitated to reach out to others. Whether with questions, words or a soothing, concerned touch, she'd always been ready to offer comfort to others.

To be interested in them. To be curious about those around her.

Many compared Robbie's wife, Sheena, to Glynnis in this regard, but Glynnis had learned it as a skill while Sheena came by it as a part of her being. And in learning it well, it had become part of her nature. Part of everything she did. How she lived. How she served.

He glanced up and found her waiting.

'Not often now,' he said. 'My duties keep me closer to Achnacarry and Tor.' Placing the chisel and wood down, he brushed the dust from his hands and leaned against the table. 'More lately because of the repairs and work on the mill.'

Iain wanted to tell her he still carved little figures, even while not here. He wanted to explain how he built this place and how no one had ever been here with him, until her. He wanted to describe his work on the mill. But he did not.

He wanted her to ask him.

And that was something she clearly was not ready to do. In truth, it was more that she could not do it than chose not to.

'The light is fading, Glynnis. 'Tis probably best if I take you back to your cottage now.' After glancing towards the door, where the change was apparent through the scant inch of opening, Glynnis nodded.

Iain put out the lanterns and opened the door to leave. Looking around the chamber, now made somehow different by her presence, he walked out and pulled the door closed. She'd waited for him there and he held out his hand to her. The hesitation was half a heartbeat long, but enough that he noticed. Still, she placed her hand in his. It took no time at all to mount, this time with her sitting behind him. When her arms encircled his waist, he tapped his heels and used the reins to guide his horse to the path and back to her cottage.

Even though the sun slid its way down the western sky, Iain did not rush their return. The wind through the trees and the splashing of the water at the edge of the loch accompanied their silent ride back. He was glad of that, for the feel of her body at his back, the way her hands clutched at his belt to keep her seat and the occasional touch of her face resting against his back robbed him of words. Words that could be dangerous to give voice to since so much depended on the expectations the clan, his chieftain, his parents and others had of him.

Expectations he'd accepted. Expectations that would result in an advantageous marriage to a woman who was not the one with him now. Honour required that he respect the boundaries between them, no matter what affections threatened to rise as he'd spent time with her.

The cottage came into view and their approach was noted for the maid walked out to greet her mistress. He eased his mount to a stop and helped Glynnis slide down, remaining where he was. She lifted her face to look at him and gifted him with a brief smile and a nod. It was not the smile he wished to see, but it was a sign to him that she was not as unaffected by their time together as she'd been just weeks ago.

'Have ye taken a chill?' the lass asked as she

draped a woollen shawl over Glynnis's shoulders, not interested in waiting on the lady's reply. 'I have some stew kept warm for ye.' She threw a disdainful glance at Iain for being the one responsible for her lady missing her meal. 'Come ye in now.'

He sat and watched as the two went inside, hearing the latch drop before he moved away. From the low angle of the sun, he would make it back to the keep before the gates closed. He could always stay at his mother's house in the village if need be. If he hurried, there would be time enough.

As he rode through the forest towards the path leading home, his hand drifted to his sporran where the carving she'd held in her hand now lay. Remembering the way she'd stroked the wood as she turned it over in her palm, Iain knew for certain that he would finish it. His flesh reacted immediately to the image in his thoughts of her touching his work so.

No matter how many times he admitted that seeing her again, allowing the memories of what they'd been to rise, and seeking to help her recover from this condition were all very bad ideas, it did not seem to silence the call in his blood. Or calm the fierce arousal he could not ignore.

Over the next day his new duties kept him busy and away from the cottage in the woods, but Iain did not fool himself into believing this would proceed easily. Or that his recurring visits to her would not be discovered.

So, the summons to the chieftain's chamber the next evening after supper did not surprise him at all.

* * *

'Come in.' Iain opened the door at Robert's call.

He knew Robert had some matter to discuss with him and he suspected he also knew the topic the chieftain wished to consider. Pushing the door to the large chamber used by the chieftain for carrying out the clan's business, he was surprised to see the others there. And their identities and presence confirmed that Glynnis was their concern. Or seeing his mother and stepfather next to the chieftain and his lady made it clear that his knowledge of Glynnis was the matter before them.

'My lord,' Iain said, nodding at Robert. 'My lady.' He lowered his head to Lady Elizabeth. 'Mother. Davidh.'

'Sit,' Robert said. He motioned Iain to a seat at the large table, where cups already awaited them. 'Elizabeth?' Robert's tone and concerned gaze as he looked at his wife was the first clue to the connection of the lord and lady's public disagreement with the woman in the woods. The lady sat in the chair her husband indicated and his mother and Davidh joined them.

An uncomfortable silence built around them, but Iain did not speak first. It was not his place nor his meeting. It did not take more than the length of several breaths for his chieftain to begin.

'I did not agree with my wife's decision to invite Lady Glynnis here, but 'twas done before I was consulted. Her intentions were the best, but I fear we did not consider all the consequences of her stay. We had hoped that you would not discover her here.'

'Robert!' Lady Elizabeth said in a furious whisper.

'Iain, she is my goddaughter and in need. I offered her a place of refuge and safety. And I tried to protect her dignity and privacy in making the arrangements.'

The lady picked up and drank deeply from her cup before continuing. Her offer to Glynnis was truly no surprise to him, for Elizabeth MacSorley, Lady Cameron, was loyal and protective to those in her care, as Glynnis had been.

Though he did not know how his knowledge of Glynnis had become known to Robert, one look at his mother's expression told him it had not been her. In truth, it made no difference how he'd found out for Iain had not hidden his actions to protect himself, he'd done it to protect Glynnis. If ever a woman wanted to hide, she was that one.

'My lord,' Iain said, 'why did you not simply tell me of her arrival? I still ken not the cause of her distress, but I would help her however I might.'

'Your past with her, Iain,' Davidh said. 'You were young and idolised her when she left. We did not wish to...'

Davidh's complete loyalty lay with his chieftain. If he suspected that Iain held conflicting feelings in his position as tanist, Davidh would not have hesitated to share those concerns with Robert. It was his way. And everyone here understood that.

'Dredge up the past,' Iain finished his stepfather's words. He stood and approached Robert, meeting his gaze. 'I have given my word to serve you and the clan as tanist, my lord. I have accepted, in good faith, the marriage arrangements you are negotiating for me. Glynnis's presence here has not changed my commitment at all in this matter.' He knelt and held out his hands to his chieftain. 'I give you my word on this.'

Iain meant every word he spoke. Too much of his life had been spent dreaming of the chance that Robert Cameron had offered—and too many hours and days and weeks since that offer had been put into being ready and deserving of that chance—to let it slip away. Something terrible had happened to Glynnis. He wished to help her, but there was nothing more than that simple human compassion between them.

'And I accept your word, Iain.' Robert accepted Iain's gesture of fealty by placing his hands over the younger man's for a moment. Then he stood and pulled Iain into a hug. 'I wanted there to be honesty between us and have this settled.'

''Tis settled for me, my lord.' Iain looked at the lady. 'I thank you for your concern, Lady Elizabeth. I just hope that Lady Glynnis recovers from her travails.'

Instead of the usual gracious reply he'd expect from the lady who'd been instrumental in his training and acceptance these last years since his arrival in Achnacarry, he watched as she pressed her lips into a thin line as if to keep from speaking. Was it a remnant of her disagreement with her husband? Anger at his discovering of her hidden goddaughter? Or something else?

'Is there anything else you require?' he asked of Robert.

'Nothing else, Iain. Anna. Davidh. I bid you goodnight.' Robert stood and held out his hand to his wife before leading her to the door. 'On the morrow,' he said, over his shoulder.

Iain followed them, needing only to turn in the opposite direction from their chambers at that last corridor to reach his own when the lady's whisper reached him.

'Honesty, Robert? Is that what you call honesty?'

The door closed with more force than necessary and Iain was left staring back down the corridor at the lady's words.

The disagreement between the lord and lady did not bode well for the clan…or for him, from the sound of it.

Chapter Seven

Glynnis would remember the moment when she realised she was indeed feeling improved, both in body and spirit. The more mundane part of it was the return of her unremarkable monthly courses, a relief after the last one. Then, one morning, as Maggie prepared for her now customary walk to the mill, Glynnis wanted to accompany her maid.

Maggie's response—her eyes blinking rapidly and her hand making the sign of the Cross several times—spoke of how unusual such a desire was. Yet she did not allow her maid's attempts to dissuade her to succeed. As the day was a warm one even this early in the hours, Glynnis walked out of the cottage without a cloak and with a sense of boldness she'd not felt in a very long time. Her body, strengthened by the miles of walking she'd done since those early days here, moved with ease now.

The path to the mill was known to her, for she spent most of her time avoiding it in her journeys around the area. Stepping on to the road that led directly to it, a tremble shook through her—which Maggie noticed.

'I can fetch yer cloak, my lady,' she said, glancing past Glynnis to the cottage still in view.

'Nay, Maggie.' Glynnis smiled, waking up muscles in her face that had not stretched in use in too many months. 'I am not chilled. Just…' The word she wanted to describe how she felt would not come to mind. 'Let us go.'

Maggie took her smile as permission to practise her newest habit—to prattle—and so the lass did. By the time the mill came into sight, Glynnis had heard more than she could have imagined she needed to know about the miller, his wife, children and especially about his handsome son. If she did not pay heed, the girl might find something more interesting to keep her here than to accompany Glynnis home.

Home.

A piece of overgrown tree root, sticking up through the mossy ground, managed to get in her way in that moment and she stumbled a bit. Maggie gasped and reached for her, but Glynnis was able to right herself. Walking faster, eyes up, and her first steps resulted in near catastrophe! She needed to have a care for her own actions before she worried over her maid's. Maggie recovered as well and began to chatter about this and that and who and what as they walked along. While all Glynnis could think about was…home.

And that brought on confusion, for she'd lived in a number of places since she'd been old enough to foster with others and did not have clear memories of the place where she'd been born and raised until her mother had died. So, was home the place she'd been born? Or the one where she'd grown up and developed her skills and fallen in love? Or was it the place where she'd lived with her husband as she desperately tried to bear him children and to live up to the expectations of his family? Or would it be wherever she moved next? Considering the changes in her life and ones that would come soon was a new experience for her. Her thoughts had been so empty for so long. Now it seemed that was changing, too.

At Maggie's silence, Glynnis looked up and saw the mill and the miller's house next to it before them. Both buildings were made of stone, the mill larger than the house as it stood astride the rushing stream that powered it. A small group of men stood talking among themselves next to the water, pointing at parts of the grindstone housing now and nodding between themselves.

Her feet stopped and an urge to change direction and flee into the trees filled her. She'd not thought about letting her presence be known to others other than the few who'd had to know, either by Lady Elizabeth's own arrangements or by necessity. Realising her possible misstep, Glynnis tugged Maggie to a stop and led her into the shadows.

'Come, I have made a mistake.' Maggie followed her. 'Lady Elizabeth ensured my presence here would not be discovered. Without kenning who is there working at the mill, her efforts may come undone and I will be to blame.'

The path through the trees was familiar so they made their way around to the far side of the mill and waited to see if the men would remain there or leave. Most of them did. All but one man. Peeking through the dense branches, Glynnis recognised him immediately. As he smacked James on the back and strode to the water's edge to examine…something, she could not tear her gaze away.

When he straightened up and began undressing, she gasped loudly enough to gain Maggie's attention. Waving off the lass, she watched as he pulled off the plaid wrapped around his waist and chest and when he tugged his tunic over his head, the breath left her. His boots were next, leaving only his breeches in place. Iain called out to James, pointing to a part of the wheel that would eventually turn the millstones, and dived under the water.

She found herself counting the moments until he broke through the surface. Words were exchanged between the two men and he disappeared once more. This was repeated several more times, her breath pausing each time. Glynnis gathered her control and forced herself to breathe. A chuckle crept out, laughing at her own reaction to seeing him. She was a married, well, widowed, woman who had seen men thus—warriors training, men working, her husband—so the sight of one man without his tunic should not shock her.

Glancing across the distance once more, she looked upon the muscular back on which she'd rested her face as they rode. The definition of those muscles, the inherent strength there and the way they had felt as he moved as he controlled the huge horse beneath them. Iain walked from the water and

Glynnis's mouth went dry. The water sluicing down his body outlined all his masculine angle and followed the path from his broad chest, across his narrower waist and hips and down again until it slipped into the loosened trews.

Her body awakened in that moment from its empty, dormant slumber. Feelings too long absent flowed through her, filling her with a need stronger than she'd experienced in such a long time. As she watched him lift his arms up and twist the water from his hair, Glynnis wanted.

Startled by all of it—her indecorous scrutiny of his half-naked body, the growing awareness within her and the inappropriateness of that—Glynnis turned away and met the somewhat horrified gaze of her maid. Though if asked what the girl was horrified by, Glynnis would be unable to say if the sight of Iain rising from the water or if witnessing her mistress ogling him had done it.

Deciding that retreat was the wisest action to make at this point, Glynnis had taken two steps towards the path leading to the cottage when the miller's voice rang out, stopping her.

'Lady…Clara! Good morrow to ye,' he called out. His hesitation in that last second revealed that he knew her true name. Had his wife or Iain shared it with him?

It was too late to escape or hide, so she inhaled and released a deep breath and turned to face the miller, the mill and Iain.

'James,' she said as they approached. 'Good morrow to you, Iain.'

'Ah, so ye hiv met the tanist then, Lady?' the miller asked. He winked as he made a somewhat valiant effort to keep up the charade.

'Aye,' they both replied, a bit more forcefully than either probably had planned to and the man's eyes widened a bit before he lowered his gaze and nodded.

'If ye are looking for Coira, she is within,' he said. 'Maggie kens the way.'

A quick peek in Iain's direction revealed he was watching her closely, even as he tugged his tunic over his head and down his torso. It had been all she could do not to stare as they'd walked up to the two men and it was almost a relief that he was covered now.

'Aye. I will seek her out,' she said, turning away and walking towards the stone cottage. By the time they reached the door, Coira stood waiting for them, drying her hands on a long length of cloth as she greeted them.

'Good day, Lady. Come in. Come in. I hiv some porridge in the pot if ye hiv not broken yer fast.'

Glynnis turned back just as she stepped inside and noticed Iain still watching her. Had he seen the heat in her eyes as she'd looked at him? The same heat that filled his gaze now? She hurried past Coira, who'd held the door open for her. Being a summer's day, leaving it ajar would allow cooling breezes to ease the heat that would build from the day's cooking and chores.

'A fine-looking man, that one,' the miller's wife whispered as Glynnis walked by her. 'He's grown up well.'

Glynnis could not help the rusty bark of a laugh

that escaped her as Coira joined in. Maggie looked at them both, having not heard the comments Coira kept to only themselves. As one married woman to another.

Of course Coira knew. A brief memory of the kind woman speaking to her during waves of pain reminded Glynnis that the miller's wife had tended to her in her time of need. And the practical woman missed nothing, not even the impressive changes in the lad who was now a man. Another recently awakened need arose, one spurred on by the aromas wafting through the woman's kitchen of well-cooked food, and Glynnis's belly grumbled loudly. She followed Coira to the table. Her appetite, once gone for months, seemed to be firmly back in place and on the increase with each passing day.

'I have not broken my fast, Coira. If you have enough to share,' she said.

'Plenty, my lady. Plenty.'

Soon, a large wooden bowl of steaming porridge—thick and creamy—sat before her and Glynnis savoured the moment when her stomach made it known it was empty. With each spoonful, Glynnis could almost feel her body strengthening from its nourishment. As she scooped the last bit into her mouth and swallowed it, Glynnis felt…

She felt.

That was what made this day different—her senses, her emotions, her body, all began to wake. That was how it seemed to her. She was waking from a long, deep sleep and becoming aware of the world and people around her. And aware of herself.

And in some ways, all the tiny steps towards her recovery felt as though they were building to this.

'That was delicious, Coira. My thanks.'

''Tis the same as I make every morn, but I think it always tastes better hot out of the pot, my lady.' Coira reached for the empty bowl even while moving the steaming bread and fresh butter closer. 'Do ye want more?'

'Nay, I have eaten my fill.' Glynnis leaned back against the chair and nodded. 'I had not been hungry in a very long time.' The sympathy in the woman's eyes stopped her. 'My appetite has only recently returned,' she finished.

'Yer looking weel this morn and ye walked here, so that is something,' Coira said, smiling and nodding. 'Taking wee steps wi' get ye along the path, too, my lady.'

Coira moved about, clearing the table, stirring the pot and such, as Glynnis realised that the chances were this woman had lost bairns as she herself had. Carrying and birthing bairns was the most dangerous thing women did and not many got through their childbearing years without a loss.

'You ken?'

'Aye, my lady. I remember ye from yer time here before,' Coira admitted. 'When I saw ye at the cottage, when ye were ailing so, I didna ken ye. But ye are looking as yer old self now and anyone who kenned ye before will ken ye now.'

So, her time here unknown in her shelter in the forest was over? She should speak to Lady Elizabeth before more discovered her. Discretion was something important to both of them.

'Would you be able to get a message to Lady Elizabeth for me, Coira?'

'I can give your message to the lady.'

Glynnis turned to find Iain standing in the open doorway, now fully dressed. His hair, yet damp from his time in the water, hung loosely around his neck and shoulders. Before she could say more, Coira spoke first.

'Come in now,' Coira said around her. 'Ye must be hungry after all yer work this morn.' Coira placed a new bowl, one easily twice the size of the one Glynnis had eaten from, in front of a stool at the table and another on the other side. 'Is my James behind ye?'

'Aye, my love, I am.' Glynnis's gaze caught Iain's for a scant moment at the endearment spoken so freely.

'Well, sit ye down and eat. There's more work to be done.'

Cups of ale and more bread were placed before the men, who wasted not a moment or a mouthful devouring the thick porridge—that she already knew was delicious—and drinking the ale. Coira busied herself around the kitchen. Glynnis tried not to stare or look too intently or too long at Iain, but realised he was simply too close to her to avoid it. So, she stood and walked nearer to the hearth and though now not watching, she listened none the less.

'Have ye finished the repairs?' Coira asked as she filled their cups from a pitcher. 'All of them?'

'We have,' Iain said. James joined him in a laugh.

'After weeks of work, correcting the damage and then correcting our mistakes, 'tis done.'

'So now Iain returns to his duties at the chieftain's side and I go back to milling grain,' James added. Maggie had explained that James had seen to milling extra flour for weeks in anticipation of these extensive repairs. Now Iain would go back to his usual schedule and pace.

As tanist. Planning his future. Preparing to lead the clan some day.

Even as she prepared for whatever future her father would plan for her. Without the bond of bairns to keep her, she had no place with her husband's family. And with *that* history, little place anywhere a man needed an heir.

As tanist, Iain would need to marry and have heirs.

That sudden realisation made her suck in a breath and glance over her shoulder at him. Through her weeks here and their many encounters, she'd never once asked him the obvious questions. In the dark fog of despair, she'd not even thought of the questions. Now, others began crowding into her thoughts.

Obvious ones—was he married or betrothed yet? How did he come to be named tanist over his older cousin Tomas? How had he risen? What had he learned? Did reading come easier to him now than it had three years ago?

Subtle ones—what were his favourite experiences in the journey he'd taken so far? Had he travelled with Robert to other places, other clans?

And finally, even personal ones—was his mother proud? Did she offer counsel in the same way she al-

ways did? What did his stepfather think of him stepping into what should have been his father's place?
How had Robbie reacted to all of this, being the cat-
alyst for much of it?

Glynnis excused herself as the closeness of the
walls and other people seemed to press in on her as
these queries exploded in her thoughts. Overwhelmed,
she fled to the edge of the stream and watched the
wheel catch up water and deposit it into the opening
that fed the gears and stones. Over and over, consistent and smooth, moving with the flowing force of the
stream, it allowed her to find her balance. She did not
have to look to know that the crunching sound of boots
on the leaves and twigs brought him to her.

'I have been asleep, Iain. For many weeks, months
even, asleep while moving through life.' She turned
and faced him, even as the questions fought against
her control. 'Unable to face the challenges that met
me. Unable to accept the constant barrage of living
and unwilling to end it.'

'Glynnis,' he whispered. She'd shocked him with
an admission she'd shared with none but him. He
reached out to take her hand, but she shook her head
and stepped away.

'Would you let Lady Elizabeth know that I would
appreciate speaking to her at her convenience?'

He studied her face, looking for more, more that
was yet impossible to say or explain despite this mo-
mentous step forward. 'That is the message you wish
given to her?'

'Aye.' Her godmother would understand that just

sending the message *was* the message in and of itself. An acknowledgement of change.

He turned and walked back inside without another word. She heard him take leave of the miller and his wife. The sound of his horse galloping away. When Coira called to her, Glynnis went back inside and watched as Maggie gathered up foodstuffs Coira had made for them into a sack to bring back to the cottage. Soon, the two were back on the road leading away from the mill.

It would be days before the lady could arrange for them to meet, so there was time for Glynnis to prepare herself for the questions her godmother would have.

At least she hoped there would be.

Chapter Eight

'You look so much better than when I saw you last, Glynnis,' her godmother said. 'And I am glad of it. Heartily.' The older woman sat in the chair next to her and patted her hand. 'But looking better does not always mean feeling well.'

'I am feeling better,' Glynnis admitted. 'I'm able to walk to the loch and the mill and back now.' She stood and paced across the small space. She stopped before Lady Elizabeth. 'Allowing me to stay here, undisturbed, has done that.'

'You've had visitors.'

'Aye. The miller and his family. They have taken good care of my needs.' But Glynnis sensed the lady meant someone else.

'Iain visits you here.' Not a query. A statement.

'He has. He discovered my presence here when I was…ill and Coira called Anna.' Glynnis met the woman's knowing gaze. 'He is much changed in these last years.' She sat once more on the chair.

'Aye. Matured into a wonderful young man,' the

lady said. 'An able successor when the time comes, and an excellent tanist now. An unexpected turn to the way I thought the matter would go, if truth be told.'

'Robbie?'

'And you, at one time, my dear.' The woman sighed. 'I pray you do not think less of me for not seeing the truth of it before he forced us to see it.'

Robbie had thought he'd hated Sheena for so long, he'd convinced himself and his family of it. It had taken Glynnis a short time to see the love—denied, ignored and fought against—developing between the two of them. It had been remarked that Glynnis would have made The Cameron's heir the perfect wife, but she knew that Sheena was the perfect woman for Robbie.

'But your father saw your value and arranged a marriage for you.'

'And he will once again,' Glynnis said.

'He will. 'Tis the way of things for women of value.'

Lady Elizabeth stared at her as she spoke. Her words seemed determined to draw a response from Glynnis. Her father understood that Glynnis's value diminished with each unsuccessful pregnancy and that her worth as a wife now stood much lower than even when she was untried. She rose from the chair and walked to the open door, staring off to the shadows of the forest.

No nobleman in search of sons would want her to wife.

No heir needing his own would marry her.

Nay, her only choices would be widowers with

children to be raised. Or a marriage needed for the alliance only with nothing else dependent on it than the bond.

Surely her godmother understood the basic facts of her situation. She'd kept in touch with Elizabeth for years, both before and after her fostering at Achnacarry. No one knew more of what had happened than the wife of The Cameron. Glynnis did not doubt that the lady knew more than even her father did.

'Are you well enough to return now, Glynnis?' The woman approached her and touched her shoulder. 'I can see that your body is healing well now, but what about the rest? Can you face your father and his demands now?'

The demands? The next marriage.

She shrugged, not knowing the answer. Though emotions seemed to be returning to her empty soul and body, could she submit to her father's wishes and another man's expectations?

'Is there a choice, my lady?' Accepting the hard reality facing her seemed to be her godmother's intent in this discussion. 'I have as much choice now as I did three years ago or even seven years ago in the decision that sent me to you.'

The lady took her hand and pulled her closer. Tears, tears, welled up and trickled down her cheeks. She'd had no idea that when feelings returned, the hopelessness would, too. Glynnis had mistaken emptiness for that lack of belief that she could live again after all of the losses had torn her apart and crushed her asunder.

As the pain filled her, she understood. She understood.

She could not pick and choose which feelings she could allow back into her heart and soul. The bad ones were coupled with the good ones as tightly as any vow or bond. To feel joy fully, one must suffer the sadness. To experience the fullness of happiness, regret and pain must have been there first. To truly celebrate living, loss must be endured.

If there was any hope of a satisfying path ahead for her, she must risk the danger of exposing herself to all it offered, with no guarantees. Elizabeth said nothing but held on to her, offering support in the silent gesture.

That was not true. Elizabeth had spoken clearly and often as she'd supported her through it all—when her betrothal to Robbie turned out to be more transient than believed and when she remained there—not kin but more an outsider looking in. Always welcoming. Always gracious to her in spite of Glynnis's lack of position and place.

This respite, arranged by Elizabeth at great cost, she suspected, was the ultimate gift. It did not give a choice in the next part of her life, but it had given her a chance to find herself again. To breathe and to rest. To feel.

Dare she give the answer she wanted to? Could she grab a bit more time? Should she beg to remain now that she wanted more? More time. More knowledge. More of a chance.

And, at the core, she wanted the opportunity to learn more about Iain.

Oh, there could be nothing between them except what had been all those years ago—an innocent, naive longing they might have called love. She would treasure those times, those feelings, but they were gone for ever now. Much like the last three years would live only in her memories.

'I have a suggestion that I would like you to consider, Glynnis,' Elizabeth said as she took a step away. 'I have not received word of your father's return from England yet. Take a few more days here before you come to Achnacarry and await his summons.'

'Achnacarry?'

'As a guest,' she explained. ''Twould be a reasonable place for you to stop on your way home. And no one would be the wiser about your stay here.' The lady glanced around the cottage. 'Well, no one who kens will speak of it.'

If being inside the miller's house with just a few people had made her uncomfortable, what would being inside the keep with dozens nearby at all times do to her? Could she do that?

'Do you not think it would be easier to begin among friends here than strangers in your father's house?' the lady asked.

'What do they ken of me?' Glynnis asked. 'Do they ken about…?' Martainn. The pregnancies. The bairn. Her stomach clenched and her heart hurt.

'They will ken only what we put out about you. News of Martainn's passing is not common knowledge here, yet, but that much should be shared. Though the Camerons and Campbells are not closely allied, Robert did send messages to their chieftain about his death.' Elizabeth met her eyes and waited.

'Aye.'

That much being known openly would make it easier to explain…her need to return home and to be here. Only Anna and Lorna, and Elizabeth herself, knew about the bairn. The news of Martainn's death would have overshadowed any other. If he had survived, her other loss would have been magnified.

'So you will…visit?'

More unwanted emotions flooded her—worry, fear, sadness—but under it all was a different feeling. One of relief. Relief at not having to keep up a charade. To keep herself secret and secreted. Relief that Iain would not have to hide their conversations in the shadows of the forest or in distant glades where they would encounter no one.

Relief that she might gain answers to all those recently risen questions.

'Aye, my lady,' she said. 'I will visit Achnacarry on my way home.'

A week later, after thanking Coira and her family for their care and help, Glynnis climbed up on her horse for the first time since she'd arrived here. With an escort arranged by Lady Elizabeth and with Maggie trailing behind, she rode through the village of Achnacarry, through the gates and up to the keep.

'We have a visitor,' Geordie said, staring past Iain as he inspected his horse's repaired shoe.

Iain straightened and turned to watch the small

group approach the door of the keep. As Geordie whistled, Iain recognised them. Her. He recognised her.

'Could that be the MacLachlan lass?' Geordie asked, stepping next to Iain as they both watched. 'I mean Lady Glynnis,' he said, nudging Iain with his elbow as he corrected his words.

'That would be Lady Campbell now,' Iain said. 'Are we done?' The need to follow her to find out what she was doing here after weeks of hiding urged him on.

'Ye are done here. Get out of my way so I can do my work, lad,' Geordie said.

One of his first chores on settling here in the village was mucking out stalls, so the old man still treated him as though he was that lad of ten-and-three instead of a man now. Between Lachlan and Geordie, they had seen to his adjustments into the established way of things here in Achnacarry, teaching him more than just woodworking and horses. Then, when it was revealed that his father had been Malcolm Cameron, only son of the old Cameron chief and heir until his murder, Davidh took over guiding him even as Robert oversaw his training as a Cameron warrior. So, he accepted Geordie's lack of respect for Iain's new position, for the man had done so much for him.

Iain crossed the yard and made it to the steps just as the small group drew to a stop. Before any of the men accompanying her could dismount, he was at her side.

'Lady Campbell, welcome back to Achnacarry,' he said as he reached up to help her to the ground. He slid his hands around her waist and lifted her down. 'I am surprised to see you here.' Her eyes widened for a moment followed by a strained smile.

''Tis good to be back,' she said in that polite voice. The one which told him nothing. The one she had mastered long ago while ignoring the other part of his words. Before he could ask her once more about her arrival, the door to the keep opened and the chieftain and the lady walked out to greet her.

The timing told him that this had been arranged. Their greetings were all perfectly spoken. Their smiles and clasped hands all part of a planned performance for anyone, everyone, watching. Glynnis stepped back from him, his hands releasing her from his hold. With a glance at him before she turned away, Glynnis made her way to her godmother, stopping to curtsy before her and Robert.

'Glynnis, I am glad you accepted my invitation,' the lady said, taking Glynnis's hand and drawing her to her side. 'How do you fare?'

Their heads leaning close, the women chatted as they walked inside, leaving him there at the bottom of the steps and Robert at the top. Robert nodded his head in their direction and Iain climbed quickly to follow along. Curious at the change of events, he wanted to speak with his chieftain to discover what had brought Glynnis to Achnacarry.

Lady Elizabeth had already led Glynnis to a small alcove where several chairs sat in an arrangement in front of one of the hearths. A small repast was waiting there—another confirmation that this was not spontaneous. Was Robert angry over this? He'd made his displeasure clear before, in front of many of those who lived within the keep that day, even if most knew not the reason as he did.

He reached them just as Robert spoke to Glynnis.

'I sent condolences to your husband's father, Glynnis, but did not send them to you at the time. I hope you ken that I, that we, are sorry for your loss, my dear.'

The words, a simple offer of sympathy, struck him dumb in its revelation. Glynnis had suffered a loss. One of such gravity she'd ended up recovering from it in the private place arranged by her godmother. And now, here she was, passing through.

Going home with no husband in sight.

With no husband.

He did not mean to gasp as the truth of her situation became apparent and the sound drew her attention to him. And there in her pained gaze he saw the truth she'd never told him.

'I, too, offer my condolences on your loss, Lady Glynnis,' he said, lowering his head towards her. Since only the chieftain and his wife were close enough to hear his words, he continued, 'I did not ken that was what brought you here.' Another flash of pain burned in her eyes, making him suspect there was so much more to this sad story than she would say.

A stiff nod was all he got in reply, but he did not expect anything else. Iain stepped back, as Robert whispered something to his wife before nodding to him and heading towards the chamber off the hall.

Her husband was dead. The loss had left her an empty shell, broken and clearly broken-hearted. Left her physically ill, so much so that his own mother had to tend to her.

Glynnis must have loved him very deeply to suffer so much at his loss.

Iain followed his chieftain, as more truths struck him.

Robert knew about Glynnis's reasons for being here, but he had not wanted her here. Robert's expression as they faced one another across the table told Iain he was correct—his chieftain had kept the news of Glynnis's situation from him a-purpose. Had kept her presence here a secret, only speaking of it when he discovered that Iain had been spending time with her.

Risking the newly set betrothal with the King's kinswoman

'So, you did not trust me, Robert?' Iain stood, hands on hips, facing down a man he'd admired. A man he'd sworn to serve.

Robert began to speak, to argue from the look of his expression, and then he held his hands up and nodded. 'Nay, I did not.'

Iain reeled back, hurt and angry and stunned by his chieftain's words. No matter what he'd said or done these last years, he'd yet to prove himself to Robert? It made no sense. He'd done nothing to cause such distrust. He'd sworn. He'd promised. He'd carried out orders. He'd supported Robert even if he had misgivings or did not understand the reasons behind his actions.

Iain found himself striding through the hall, heading for the stairway that led to the lower level of the keep, before he realised he'd taken a single step. Along the corridor and out through the door that led directly to the yard. Once there, he looked around at the other outbuildings, seeking…something. Seeing nothing that made sense to him, he walked to the far corner of the enclosed bailey and leaned back on the stone wall. From this place and position, he could take in all of Achnacarry Castle—its keep, the yard, the stables, storehouse and its people.

He'd given his all, every ounce of himself, to learn how to serve his father's clan. Yet, for some reason, it had not been enough for Robert. Even while the man proclaimed his support and moved him closer and closer to his goal—tanist—there was still some doubt. As he stood there, lost in his thoughts, one thing struck him.

Glynnis *was* a weakness for him.

The one person who'd made him consider running away. The person whom he'd spent time with and seen while attempting to keep their encounters hidden or, at the least, kept from his laird's knowledge. But for Davidh's keen eye and knowledge of him and his complete loyalty to Robert, it might have remained unknown.

A weakness that his chieftain had recognised. One his stepfather had as well. Only he had not realised the danger in a hidden weakness.

Leaning his head on the rough, cold stone, he knew he had not kept faith with Robert after all. And that he must make it right. A man must right the mistakes he made. A noise drew his attention and he followed the sound of it, up and up, until he spotted Robert up on the battlements.

He'd made mistakes in the past and he'd faced them. He'd made them with Robert, including the night when drink took his wits and had him spouting all sorts of nonsense to everyone in the hall and at the laird's table. And each time, Robert extended him patience rather than striking out as was his right. Iain had heard stories of the previous chieftain and his ruthless, cruel ways and understood his own existence would have been in danger with that man if Iain's parentage had been known. Gilbert would have killed anyone who stood in the way of his claim.

As Iain, son of Malcolm Cameron, would.

Staring across the distance as Robert spoke to the guards there on the heights, Iain understood he must make this right. To have the type of trust that Davidh had with his chieftain took work, on both sides. So, he must do the same to gain Robert's faith. He stood and made his way to where Robert stood, waiting for him to finish his discussion with the two guards. He sent them off with a nod of his head and turned to face Iain.

'I—' He truly did not know what to say.

'You arrived here in Achnacarry just a year after I claimed the high seat on my brother's death.' Iain was ten-and-three when he moved here, and though aware of the turmoil within the clan's leaders, he'd never heard the whole of it. 'Too young to have a care about who came when or what.' Robert smiled. 'And so caught up in holding control, I never did notice the resemblance of yours to my elder brother Euan or his long-dead son.'

Robert turned back to the edge of the stone battlement and leaned his arms there, glancing around the area beneath them. The yard was always busy at this time of day and this place had a good view of its many parts and what was going on in most of them. Only the other side of the keep was out of view.

'Has anyone told you how I became chieftain, Iain? Your mother was not here either, but mayhap Davidh revealed the whole of it to you?'

'Only that your brother had plotted against his own kith and kin in a devil's bargain and he was challenged and killed by your stepson. And that you took the seat as next in line.'

Robert laughed, but did not face him.

'So, Davidh has not revealed the rest of it?' Iain could not think of what Davidh could have held back. Or what he had not heard in gossip or talk in these years since his arrival.

'I do not ken, my lord.'

'I suspect that no one wants to ruin the fine opinion you have of us.' His words shocked Iain. At this moment, he could not comprehend a way that Robert could shake his high opinion of his clan chieftain.

'He was my younger brother, Iain. Gilbert should never have had the high seat of the Camerons when our brother, your grandfather, died. But I had a weakness and it allowed him to control me for years.'

'A weakness, my lord? What could he use against you?'

Robert was honourable, brave, sensible and loyal.

What could he have done? Iain tried to remember any rumours about Robert back when he'd arrived here. Other than the man helped Davidh rescue him from outlaws intent on using him against the Camerons, he could think of nothing else.

'The same weakness you have, Iain. The same one,' he said. 'Robbie tried not to fall victim as I had and even he failed.' Robert did face him now. 'Love, Iain. Well, not love by itself, but failing to recognise its power over you.'

'Anything I felt for the lady ended three years ago, my lord. I give you my word on that.'

'I am not questioning your honour, lad,' Robert said. 'I accept that you sought her out believing you only wanted to help her. To help an old friend, as you have probably convinced yourself.' He paused and let out a breath. 'But unless you admit the truth to yourself, it will always be your weakness. A fault upon which you shape the rest of your life. A vulnerability that will undermine the strength of any relationship you build from now on.'

Iain wanted to argue the point, but he held the words behind his teeth. Robert was not finished.

'I made that mistake and it jeopardised the entire clan,' Robert said, his voice low and hoarse. 'I did not see all the possible consequences of choosing love over duty.' The change in his expression—desperation and loss filled his eyes for a moment and was gone— made his own gut tighten. 'I should have broken my betrothal to Elizabeth and yet I could not. In choosing to stand by her instead of choosing my duty to my clan, it gave my brother Gilbert control over the clan and over me.'

'Robert—' Iain stopped at the curt shake of Robert's head.

'Make no mistake, Iain. I would have chosen Elizabeth a thousand times over, but I did not look at it clearly, and by keeping her secret, I gave Gilbert the power to hurt her, to hurt my clan by doing so.' Iain did know that everyone thought Alan was Robert's son as well until Gilbert exposed that secret.

Robert reached over and placed his hand on Iain's shoulder. 'Denying what you felt for Glynnis places you in danger, too. Acknowledging what you two shared and moving on from it to accept your duty and your place makes it less a weakness and more a choice of your own.'

Of anything the chieftain could have said, no matter what advice or warnings he could have issued, these words, this advice, was not what he expected. To speak on a topic like that—about love—and as though it mattered in the decisions of a powerful chieftain of a mighty clan shocked Iain.

And yet, the strength of the relationship between the lord and his lady, these years later, spoke of the depth of their love. Especially if it had been at the heart of a division that had nearly split the clan.

'I will think on your words, my lord,' he said at last. 'And on how I can regain your trust.'

'Be honest with yourself first and then be honest with me. Can Lady Glynnis be used against you? Against your clan?' Iain started to speak, but Robert waved him off. 'I want no acclamations or promises from you, Iain. I want you to consider my words and we will talk later.'

Robert left before Iain could ask any of the questions that the man's words had raised. And there were many. His chieftain strode to the doorway leading to the stairs and disappeared within, leaving Iain to wonder what Robert was not saying in spite of revealing much.

Apparently, even the Cameron secrets had secrets.

Chapter Nine

Her body ached as though she'd lived one hundred years.

After the ride here from the cottage and getting settled in a chamber above-stairs, Glynnis fought to keep her eyes open through supper. And she'd thought herself ready to move back into a place filled with other people!

Lady Elizabeth maintained the charade of this being a spontaneous visit well, for it was clear from Iain's expression as she rode in that he had not known of it. He'd called her Lady Campbell as he'd helped her down so it was clear he'd not heard of her husband's death either. His shock was palpable to her as he stood a short distance away and listened to his chieftain's words.

Why had she not told him? Oh, at first she had not the strength to ask or answer questions or talk much at all. But that visit to his work croft would have been the perfect time to tell him. She leaned forward a bit and glanced down the table to where he sat, speaking intently to his stepfather and never once looking in her direction.

She'd thought better of eating the meal here in the hall, but Elizabeth had asked her to do so—and how could she refuse that simple request? Truth be told, the meals here at Achnacarry were her most favourite times. Oh, the food was plain, but always plentiful. The chieftain sat with his closest kin and joined in the discussions, no matter how unimportant or even mundane they were. She remembered meals where some of those who worked in different parts of the castle and village were invited.

There were, certainly, times when Robert and Elizabeth held formal dinners for visiting nobles or important persons from all over Scotland. But the truly best part of those gatherings were the ceilidhs, when song and dance would follow the meal and the hall filled with laughter and clapping and…joy.

'What are you thinking on, Lady Glynnis?' Tomas Cameron asked softly from across the table. 'The strangest smile just brightened your face and I am curious.'

'Tomas, we have kenned each other long enough that there is no need for "lady" between us,' she said.

Robbie's younger brother and Robert's youngest son, Tomas was a young man of even temperament and filled with a deep sense of kindness and humour. For a brief time, some had held hopes that they would marry, but once Robbie married Sheena and her father had summoned her home with his own plans, there was no possibility of it. Still, they had spent hours together over her years here and he felt more sibling to her than anything else.

'I was just remembering some of the ceilidhs held here in the hall.' She stared across the length of the hall where tables now stood while people were eating. Those tables would have been pushed aside to clear the area for dancing. A fiddler and other musicians would be seated nearest the front. Anyone who wished to dance could. No one stood on formality when it came to dancing. 'That is all.'

'We have not held one for some time now,' Tomas said. 'I am certain there will be one soon, what with—' He stopped whatever he was going to say when his mother spoke her name.

'Would you walk with me to my chambers, Glynnis?'

Glynnis stood, as did Tomas and the other men at the table, as the lady walked to her side. Sliding her arm around Glynnis's, she led her away from the table.

'You are so pale, I thought you might faint away,' the lady whispered as they passed through an archway and followed the corridor to the stairway.

'If you have need of me, my lady—'

'Nay. That was a ruse to get you away from the table and to your chamber. I did not wish to draw more attention to your distress.'

Glynnis allowed the assistance and they climbed to the floor two flights up and down to the room assigned to her. In the family tower where she'd stayed before. Losing strength with each step, she feared the lady might have been correct. With a quiet word of farewell, her godmother left her.

Maggie waited in the bedchamber for her, her clothing now taken from wherever the lady had stored it on her arrival and her maid had unpacked it, filling the cupboard in the corner and several trunks. Maggie had a talent for turning an empty chamber into a welcoming place as she had the plain little cottage in the woods and as she had made this room.

If she was to be here, at least she would be comfortable in a well-strung bed, piled high with blankets and pillows, all just calling her name and luring her to the depths of sleep. It was only as she drifted to sleep that Tomas's words repeated in her thoughts. He was certain there would be a ceilidh soon, with...

A ceilidh soon.

To...

The next thing she knew, the sun's light had been shining between the wooden shutters that covered the window high up on the wall of her chamber.

Summer storms arrived a few hours later, sending the villagers scampering for cover from the heavy, windblown rains and lightning. For some hours, darkness like night surrounded them and Glynnis could not remember such a storm as this.

Unable to go outside, she joined the lady and her maid and other companions in the solar, where the women worked on various chores and tasks. Glynnis found she enjoyed being in their company, for they seemed content to speak among themselves and not demand that she participate. Their topics changed quickly and not always smoothly, but Glynnis learned much through that morning about changes to the household and within the clan. Much was different from before.

The one topic they did not speak on was their tanist.

Elizabeth's maid shared her infatuation for one of the guards who accompanied the chieftain on his duties. From the lady's indulgent smile, Glynnis had no doubt that such a match would be supported. As the chatter continued, sometimes soft and other times more boisterous, it felt the perfect balance to the dark and dismal day outside.

'Would you like to rest?' the lady asked after the light repast of cheese and bread and an aromatic soup was cleared from the chamber.

'I think not, my lady.' In truth, she'd rested very well last night and did not feel the need to do so now. 'It does not mean I will not fall asleep at table again, but I think not.' The attempt at a bit of humour felt forced, but Elizabeth smiled and nodded.

'You must move at your own pace. No one will place any demands on your time or efforts, Glynnis.'

'Still no word from my father?' she asked. This absence from Scotland by her father was much longer than his usual sojourns to his lands in the south. So, her time here, her time without demands, must end soon.

'Robert's had no correspondence at all from him.' Her godmother shifted in her chair, handing off her needle and thread to her maid. 'Glynnis, I would speak to you about…a matter…'

Elizabeth nodded to the perceptive servants around them and they left quickly and quietly, leaving them alone. Glynnis inhaled in a measured manner, trying to resist the sense of panic that rose unexpectedly in her. Worrying had been absent within her for so long, it took several long moments to recognise it.

'Since you are here and will be among the villagers and those here in the keep, there is something you should ken.' Elizabeth leaned in closer. 'Since Iain was named tanist just before you arrived here, I doubt you know this yet.'

Even though they'd spent some time together, Iain had revealed almost nothing about his life and this new role. Well, other than that he continued on with his carving. But she'd not felt the need or necessity to reveal anything about hers either. Now, though, curiosity rose, pushing aside the first rush of trepidation.

'Robert has arranged a betrothal for Iain. One that will be of great benefit to the Camerons. One that will link him to the King's family.' Elizabeth met her gaze and watched her closely as she finished. 'One that will link the Camerons to the royal family.'

Delivered in such a quiet and balanced tone, Glynnis could not be sure that the lady supported this alliance or not. Expecting joy or happiness in such an announcement, she was more surprised to hear none of it. Or did the lady hold back on her account?

'That sounds very advantageous,' Glynnis said. 'For Iain and your family.'

It was an honest comment, for marriage to someone related to the King could bring their clan into a higher level of influence within the country. Such a marriage would have enormous benefits and give Iain opportunities he'd never have had as an unknown cousin of The Cameron. One that the Iain she'd known would never have sought or been considered for before she'd left.

'To whom is he betrothed, my lady?' The King was related to many clans and families throughout Scotland, France, England and more.

'She is called to Elen *verch* Pwyll, in the Welsh way. A cousin related to the King by his great-grandmother,' Elizabeth said. A smile lifted the corners of her mouth, a small sign of pleasure with this match. 'Descended from Llewelyn the Great of Wales.'

'The Cameron must be pleased.' Any chieftain in possession of half their wits and any measure of intelligence would be pleased. Her own father would be crowing loudly to any and all souls if he'd a son connected even in this small way to the King. Small or even tenuous connections were still useful. 'Have you or your husband met the woman yet?' That would be the customary way of it.

'Nay. The lady will come here by summer's end. If everything is as it should be…' Elizabeth paused. *If there were no significant obstacles or objections between them.* 'The marriage will be held in autumn.'

Glynnis nodded. Her godmother continued to study her, as though waiting for some outburst or questions. She did have questions, several of them swirled in her thoughts, but she would rather speak to Iain. He deserved an explanation for her silence, especially after his attempts to watch over her while she stayed in the cottage. And, she understood, for more than that. She owed Elizabeth even more.

'I will offer him my best wishes when I speak to him next,' she said. Glynnis stood, shaking the wrinkles out of her day gown as she did. 'May I take my leave of you, my lady? It looks like the rains have stopped and I would like to walk a bit.'

Her godmother stood and reached out to her for a brief moment before allowing her hand to drop. Glynnis made her way across the chamber, dropping her own embroidery in a basket by the door. She lifted the latch, waiting with each step to be called back. On reaching the corridor without another word being spoken, she turned and walked along the hallway, re-acquainting herself with the turns and corners of the keep as she made her way to the lower storey and to the door that led out to the yard.

It was hard to believe that the morning had been so dark and stormy when taking in the bright sun that now reflected off the puddles collected in div-ots and pooled in the gulley that divided the yard with its water rushing downhill. Having a care to step over and around them, she found a remembered out-of-the-way spot and watched the busyness of the keep and its surrounding buildings. Tasks that needs must be accomplished regardless of the rain would wait no longer—the keep and the yard seemed to awaken as if from a nap like the one Lady Elizabeth suggested she take.

Small groups of servants and warriors and those who worked in the stable and the kitchen and the storehouses took up their chores and duties. Except for her. Glynnis found the small alcove between the stables and the enclosed area where the warriors trained. The sunlight, now unfiltered by thick clouds, heated the ground and the areas not shaded, so she stepped back in the shadows to avoid it.

Glynnis lost herself in the sights and sounds of everyday life here, something she'd been away from for three years. Once she'd married, she'd lived at the whims and direction of her husband, his father and his mother. Expected to be the companion to her mother-by-marriage and to get on with producing heirs for her husband, her life was limited and centred. No time left on her own, to spend observing those who lived with them. With few, if any, friends and no opportunity to make them, Glynnis herself had diminished with each passing month and sorrow. When she arrived here, she was hollowed out, like a dressed deer after a kill.

She inhaled the rain-freshened air and felt it within her. Those three years and all but nothing left to boast of. Except that she'd been the perfect lady. The perfect wife. The perfect companion. Accepting direction. Following orders. Praying for bairns. And praying again. And again.

Glynnis closed her eyes and let out all this newly built frustration. Or maybe she'd just not allowed herself to feel that before? She was so intent on being the woman she'd been trained and taught to be that she'd ignored her own misgivings and needs. But that was the only way she knew to be.

And now? What did she do now?

Standing there, eyes closed, breathing in the fresh, pine-scented Highland air, she did not hear anything until he spoke.

* * *

Iain had not crept up on her. Indeed, he had strode towards her a-purpose, making no secret that he was getting closer to her. As he walked nearer, he noticed that she stood with her face lifted towards the sunny sky with her eyes closed. The sense of calm in her features as she stood there in silence made him hesitate before speaking.

He'd seen her sobbing. He'd seen her staring off into the depths of the forest. He'd watched as she'd examined every tool and part of his workbench. Each time, each encounter was like meeting a different woman from the one before and very different from the one he'd known. Or thought he had.

Iain watched her in silence, as the gentling breezes managed to lift the veil that lay over her hair and free some of her long brown curls. With her hair swirling around her face and the calm of her expression, she looked more like he remembered. At least now he understood some of the travails in her life that had caused such changes in her appearance and her manners.

She was in mourning.

Her husband, Martainn Campbell, had died just several months ago. Robert did not have many other details, but he had shared that the death was sudden and unexpected. An accident of some kind. Such a thing would have shocked her, for certain. And without children to bind her to her husband's kin, she would have needed the refuge her godmother offered.

Aye, Robert had told him that bit as well. If mother to the heir's heir, she would have been afforded a place of honour and welcome there. Without that claim…

When she let out a sigh, he knew he must speak before she discovered him standing here gawping at her.

'Does it feel strange to be back here, Glynnis?'

Her eyes opened slowly, as if rising from a deep sleep or pleasant dream, and his body reacted in a way he'd not expected. As it seemed to do with regularity when she was nigh. After blinking a few times, she nodded.

'It does, truly. Stranger here even than the cottage.'

'Sheena likes this spot when she visits.'

'I remember. Out of the way, shaded by the stables and trees. You can watch without being seen,' she said. Glynnis had been a staunch supporter of Robbie's wife upon her arrival here. She'd protected the woman from scrutiny and guided Robbie to discover what was at the heart of Sheena's difficulties. 'I have not heard from her…in some months. Is she—are they well?'

Strange that those had been Robbie's words when he'd asked about Robbie's wife contacting Glynnis. 'Aye, well enough. Robbie was here recently and said Sheena will be soon.' He shifted on his feet. 'Considering the circumstances, it's not unexpected that you lost touch.' He stepped a half-pace closer. 'I did not ken about your husband, Glynnis. Until just last evening when Robert spoke of his passing.' She gave a slight nod of acceptance of his explanation.

'I do not ken why I did not speak of it, of him, to you, Iain.' She paused to take a breath and release it. 'It has been a struggle for me these last months.' He could see that she was not the same as the first time he'd encountered her, but did not argue with her. 'But I must be on the mend, for Lady Elizabeth suggested I move here and accommodate myself to others. A step in my preparation,' she added.

'You do look stronger than the first time I saw you out at the cottage.' She sighed and glanced over his shoulder, not meeting his gaze. 'Have I offended you, Glynnis? 'Twas not my intention.'

'Nay,' she said, her soft brown eyes looking at him. 'I have struggled through these last months.' Tears shimmered there in her eyes as she spoke. 'But I am improved. Stronger.'

'I am glad of it,' he said. 'If you have need of anything from me, just say so.'

'Ah, you take your duties as tanist seriously.' A mere hint of a smile lit her face—the changes it wrought were shockingly appealing. 'Speaking of your selection as tanist,' she said, leaning closer, 'the lady told me of your betrothal this morn. I offer my congratulations on such an…an advantageous marriage.'

He'd known the way of things among nobles—that women were used as chattels and for alliances—but, for some reason, it had just struck him that he was the one being used in that way now. Somehow hearing good tidings coming from her, from a woman who had been used and would be again, made it all real.

Iain nodded, accepting her words. Although he would not deny the awkwardness he felt, it also lifted a concern from his shoulders. Each time they'd spoken, Iain had held back telling her about the betrothal.

It all led back to the choice she'd made, and though he had wanted to berate her at the time, in truth her decision had led him to this point in his life when he was the one who could choose his path.

'Are you planning to remain here secluded in the shadows or would you like to walk into the village? I have some time before I must go with Robert to Tor.'

'If you are certain you have time, I would like that.' The sound of her voice as she accepted made him smile.

They walked side by side around the stables and down through the yard until they reached the gates. Thinking on whom Glynnis might remember from her time here, Iain led her through the village until the aroma of freshly baked bread grew stronger. Though the very experienced cook in the main kitchens at the keep did most of the baking for those who lived and ate there, Finley, along with his wife, Jeannie, did most of what the villagers needed.

But Finley's talent was known far and wide and Iain knew Glynnis would remember his skill. They'd turned the corner when she inhaled deeply and smiled, a true smile, the first one since her return. His own stomach grumbled at the smell, for he frequented Finley's baking ovens often and he'd not broken his fast this morn.

'Until I smelled them just now, I'd forgotten Finley's wonderful loaves.'

'Forgotten them? Is that possible?' he scoffed. 'Well, I am certain he will have an extra one for you to refresh your memories.'

The door was open, as was his usual custom to

allow the heat of the ovens to escape, and the smell as they approached made his mouth water in anticipation. Finley's wife, Jeannie, stepped outside just as they arrived at the door.

'Good morning, Iain,' she said. 'Finley, the lad looks famished. Bring him along some bread and grab the chunk of cheese I left on the shelf for him.' She winked at him as she continued calling out over her shoulder, 'We canna hiv the tanist faint wi' hunger now, can we?'

Only then did she pause to notice Glynnis standing next to him. He was about to remind the baker's wife of the lady's identity when she stepped past him to stand in front of Glynnis.

'My lady,' she said, as she bowed her head slightly in respect. 'I hadna heard of yer arrival here. Welcome back to Achnacarry.' Once more the older woman tilted her head and spoke over her shoulder. 'Finley, Lady Glynnis is here and looks a bit peaked. Bring some fresh bread and do it now.' Jeannie leaned closer to Glynnis and whispered to her, 'Are ye weel, my lady? Ye look a wee bit pale.'

'I am well, Jeannie,' Glynnis said in the lightest tone of voice he'd heard from her. 'And I thank you for your concern.'

Finley arrived with two steaming loaves, wrapped in cloth and tucked under one arm, a wedge of cheese in his hand and a wide smile for both of them. The glance he gave his wife had as much steam as the bread did and the couple made no attempt to hide their attraction to each other—even now years after the woman married a lad years younger than she.

'Good morn, Iain. Lady Glynnis, 'tis good to see

ye again.' The baker handed out his bounty even as he slid his arm around his wife. 'If ye would like some butter for those, I hiv—'

'Nay,' Iain said. He'd already peeled open the cloth and torn a piece off the end of the loaf. Steam rose in waves from the exposed baked dough inside it. He tore another bite off with his teeth, chewing and swallowing it before saying another word.

They were very familiar with his ravenous hunger that never seemed to be satisfied completely, for he often stopped here on his way through the village. Iain turned to Glynnis and watched as she broke off smaller pieces than the chunks he had and chewed them in a manner he could only describe as…polite. But, for as long as he'd known her, she had always done that. Her best manners on display. Always the lady.

Had she ever been a hellion? Even for a few minutes or an hour? He had glimpsed those few rebellious gestures she made with him, but she would not have been condemned for any of them by anyone but herself. He watched as she spoke to Jeannie and wondered if she'd ever been drunk. Or refused some duty or chore given her. He doubted that kind of defiance lived within her.

But as he saw her struggling to continue to have a conversation and continuing to do so because of the couple's kindness to them, he understood the effort it was taking for her to engage like this. Because she would not put herself above others.

'We should not keep you from your tasks,' he interrupted. 'Others need your skills and our lives might be forfeit if we are the cause for them not having their allotment.'

Finley nodded and Jeannie waited for them to leave. By the time they'd taken a few paces away, he heard the buoyant giggles of two people playing at love. If Glynnis heard them, she gave no sign as they walked on down the path and around this side of the village. His bread and cheese were gone within the first minutes, but Glynnis had wrapped the remnants of hers back up in the cloth Jeannie had used and carried it with her. Iain took the shorter way back to the keep when he noticed her steps slowing down beside him.

He offered his arm to her and when she accepted it without comment, he felt the trembling. He'd taken her too far. And, as was her way, she'd not objected. Iain guided her up the steps and they found her maid waiting there. Just before the young woman reached them, he leaned in close so only Glynnis would hear his words.

'You must have a care, Glynnis. Know your limits. Do not let others take advantage of your willingness,' Iain said.

'My willingness?' She looked startled by his words.

'Your willingness to diminish yourself to the needs of others. Not even me.' He stepped back and allowed Maggie closer.

As the two walked away from him, Glynnis glanced back over her shoulder, a frown marring her brow. It was clear she'd never considered herself first. Or second. Or even important in the scheme of life.

And maybe she should.

Chapter Ten

The next three weeks were among some of the most contented in her life. As her godmother promised, no one made demands on her and she accepted or declined requests for her time or efforts based on her own desires.

Oh, she could not completely wipe away the need to comply or the urge to be of help. Idle hands were not part of her upbringing and the stronger she felt the harder it was to resist offering her efforts or assistance. Especially difficult considering what Lady Elizabeth and even The Cameron had done in giving her sanctuary in her time of need.

One evening after supper when most at table had sought their bedchambers, Lord Robert took her aside and spoke candidly to her of his reaction to discovering his wife's plans and assured her of his welcome of her here.

As she sat at table that evening, with the doors open to catch the summer breezes, listening to a variety of conversations, Glynnis was absolutely content.

Her body felt hers again, her strength and stamina improved each day and even her courses had seemed to right their timing. Though she mourned each time they came, even that lessened over time.

The best thing over these last weeks had been the feeling of ease she felt around all of the Camerons, with each passing day. With the long summer days, and the weather unseasonably dry and pleasant, she took advantage to walk after supper and before the gates were closed. She knew not if the lady had orchestrated it so that she did not walk alone at night or not, but somehow, someone always turned up at just the time when she would leave the keep.

Some nights, Tomas walked with her. When Robbie visited again, they walked and she was glad of the chance to reacquaint herself with him. Once his intended betrothed, they had always been on comfortable terms and a marriage with him would have been that as well. In a word—comfortable. What was clear from his words and the way his face lit with every mention of Sheena was that he was deeply in love with her and not a bit disappointed in the changes that love had wrought in his life. In the privacy of her own thoughts, Glynnis admired that, in spite of the consequences that had rippled out from his choice.

How must that feel? To have the freedom to make your own choices. To go about knowing you had that power. She let out another sigh.

'Is that boredom or fatigue?' Iain walked behind her chair. Pulling out the empty stool next to her, for Tomas had left on some errand for his father, he sat down.

'Neither,' she said. "Twas acceptance of a universal truth.'

Now that they were more at ease in speaking, she noticed all the things she'd first liked about him. Oh, some had changed—his height, his age, his position. And others had improved—his strength, his sense of humour, his loyalty. Where he'd been quiet as a younger man, now he strode through his world with confidence and with that same control over his destiny as Robbie had.

'And that truth?'

She glanced at him for a moment, tempted to reveal the truth in her heart. That she wanted more than she would ever be able to have. That she wanted to be the one to choose. But the one truth that lay deep in her heart was the one she could never reveal. Not to him.

'That is something we can discuss on another day.'

He laughed at her reply and that truth in her heart grew at the pure delight in it. It did her spirit good to see how he enjoyed his life. Each day, he grew in the respect of The Cameron and all who lived in his domain. Each week, he moved closer to attaining the life Iain wanted and, from the sound of bits shared with her, the one he was looking forward to living.

'Have you plans to walk?' he asked once he stopped laughing. When she hesitated, the knowledge within her heart too fresh and too frightening, he stood. 'I have to speak with Geordie about a forthcoming journey to Tor. Would you walk with me?'

He began to hold out his hand to her and stopped. She noticed even the small touches now that he made in passing. Every time he was near to her. Each time his hand slid under her elbow to support or guide her body. Her body reacted in a completely different manner to these gestures than it had when they were younger. At that time, she only anticipated and dreamed of the passion whispered to exist between men and women. Their innocent kisses and caresses teased and thrilled them, for both had been untested by pleasures of the flesh.

Glynnis rose, glanced and nodded at Iain, as the unsettling question took hold of her before she could stop it.

How many lovers had he taken his pleasure with since her departure?

She stumbled and he did reach out to her. To cover the misstep, Glynnis tugged on the length of her gown as though it had been trapped. Why was she thinking about that? Why now?

The heat in his touch warmed her as he made certain she had her balance. His body was so close to hers now that she felt the strength in his muscles as he kept his hand in place, not allowing her to fall. The masculine, clean scent of him drew her closer. She recognised what she was doing and stepped out of his hold.

Mayhap walking with him right now, as this unexplained weakness in her response to him surged into being, was not a good idea? Mayhap she should sit right back down in her chair and call for more ale to cool the growing heat within her? Aye, that's what she should do. Exactly that. Yet, when she spoke, she surprised herself with the words.

'I will walk with you.'

He smiled as he allowed her to go ahead of him. He moved to her side and they crossed the hall and left by means of those open doors. They fell into an even pace as they made their way to the far side of the yard and into the stables. Neither spoke, but her thoughts raced. Filled with inappropriate questions that she wanted to ask him none the less, Glynnis stood at the end of the row of stalls and watched him as he found Geordie and pursued the matter that had brought him here.

Their deep voices rumbled and the echoes filled the stables, empty but for them and the horses. Iain walked into the main aisle that ran the length of the building and turned back to Geordie, giving her a chance to study him.

Aye, Iain Mackenzie had grown into a fine-looking man. As she looked upon him, whispered words came to mind.

As a widow, I can have my pick of them for bed play, ye ken.

A strong shiver raced through her body, waves of heat and cold passing over her skin as the words came to her. Searching her memory for the identity of the one who'd spoken those words, Glynnis could hear a bit of the overheard conversation of her first days with the Campbells.

Glynnis had been walking through the kitchens and passed by a small group of servants and the like gathered by the door staring out as a number of the Campbell warriors trained outside. Looking past the women to the men training, Glynnis noted that most of them practised without their shirts, no matter the weather. Those who wore shirts were as good as naked, for their sweat plastered their garments over their bodies, showing every curve and muscle as they moved and fought.

Though new to the marriage bed and the naked forms of men, Glynnis felt the heated blush move up her cheeks as she listened...and watched along with the others.

The woman nearest the door had spoken. *As a widow, I can have my pick of them for bed play, ye ken.*

Not a servant, this woman was kin to Martainn, a cousin whose husband had served in the household. Now, widowed, she looked for companionship where she could find it and no one said much about it for she was, usually, discreet.

A widow had more freedom than either an unmarried or married woman did. If not under the control of her husband's family or her father and not expected to remarry at their whim, she could live among them and see to her own keep. Though some were permitted their freedom, her father did not agree.

Still, she was a widow here and now. She could...

Turning back to where the men stood, Glynnis found Geordie gone while Iain was watching her with an intensity that made her want him more.

She was staring at him as though he was the last sweet on the tray at the end of a feast. Her eyes flashed and her mouth dropped open, enough for him to see that she breathed in short little pants.

Hungry.

Nay, wanting.

Wanting…him?

She'd filled his dreams when they were together. His naive dreams about a love so pure it would last their lifetimes. Since Glynnis had come back to Achnacarry, she'd filled his nights in a way he knew they could never have.

And the expression she wore right in this moment was the one he'd wished for years he'd see.

And there it was.

She wanted him the way he'd wanted her. For years. Before she left him. After she'd gone. Since her return. And every other second since he'd met her all those years ago.

But he would not take what she would not give him.

Though he would beg if she needed to hear that.

Iain looked away, trying to break the power of her gaze. If he did not, he might…

Do any number of things if she came to him.

When she moved, he stopped breathing. When the tip of her tongue slid out and ran along her bottom lip, his flesh hardened.

It took only four paces for her to reach him. He counted each one as she approached. His hands clenched into fists to keep from touching her. Oh, he wanted to, but he sensed that she had no idea of her power in that moment. Or the line they would face or cross if this went the way he thought it might.

Damn him, the way he wanted it to go.

When she stood before him, close enough that his

boots touched the edge of her gown, she lifted her face to his.

'Iain.' His name was a plea on her lips.

'Glynnis, this is—'

'Unexpected,' she said. He laughed.

'Daft.'

'Aye, at least daft.' How she moved closer he could not tell, but she shifted and rose up on her toes until he could feel her breath on his face. 'I've been empty for so long, not questioning or wanting anything. Anyone,' she explained. Then she simply demanded, 'Kiss me, Iain.'

Did he think about refusing her? He might have, but he did not and the thought fled as he wrapped her in his arms and held her closer. Leaning down, he touched his lips to hers. Softly. Gently. Barely a touch. Until she sighed and canted her head. Until she opened her mouth and invited him in.

Iain slid his tongue against hers in the heat of her mouth and tasted her. He had not forgotten the sweetness of her. No matter their sad parting or the passage of time. She was sweet on his tongue. Her body leaned against his and he felt the feminine softness and curves against his hardness. His hand glided up and over her back until he could touch her hair. Pushing the veil she wore out of his way, he tangled his fingers into her braid, pulling most of it free. When her tongue rubbed against his, he arched into her, pressing his erection against her belly.

He'd been wanting this since the moment he realised she was the woman in the cottage. Against all reason and all reasons, he wanted this. He wanted her.

Pushing away the thoughts trying to force themselves in, he possessed her mouth, suckling her tongue and mimicking that act they'd never experienced together. Iain lifted his mouth a little, but she reached up and slid her hands into his hair, tugging him back.

And he went gladly.

Their bodies touched and he felt her press her breasts against him. She moaned and he deepened the kiss. Whether it was someone coming or just the sound of the breezes in the trees, a loud crack just outside startled them and he released her. As she reached up to repair her braid, he retrieved and handed her the veil he'd pulled free.

'Glynnis.'

Had he shocked her? Was this what she'd expected when she'd asked…nay, demanded, that he kiss her? As she faced him, all he could see were her swollen lips and the blush in her cheeks. When her gaze moved up to meet his, he wondered if her eyes would show the regrets she must feel for this encounter. She had asked for a kiss and he'd instead possessed her mouth as he'd dreamed about doing.

'Iain,' she said as their eyes met. She smiled.

She smiled.

As he remembered her doing in their happier times together. When she lived here and had not a care about anything. When she still had her life ahead of her. Before life and marriage. Before loss.

'I am—'

'I am not,' she said. 'But I ask your pardon if you are?'

He laughed, for what else could he do? No woman

he'd kissed had ever offered an apology…except Glynnis.

'I am not asking, Glynnis.'

She adjusted the veil and looked out into the yard, where the sun's light was fading. When he would have stepped around her, she touched his hand.

''Twas just a kiss, Iain. I understand that there can be nothing more between us. That you will marry soon and I am not suitable for…' She swallowed and glanced away. 'And I return home.' The eyes that looked at him now shimmered with a hint of tears. 'I just wanted to share a kiss with you before…all that.'

'Should we go back?' he asked, looking to see if anyone was near the doorway.

'I am not ready to return,' she said. 'Go on without me.'

Iain stopped, surprised by her words and the way she spoke them. 'If you are certain?'

She nodded and he strode away from her, fighting the urge to go back and kiss her again. And again.

His body, far different from that of the younger man she'd known and before he'd grown and trained, wanted her in a way he'd not felt before. What was between them before was something gentle and new, but what raced through him now was nothing like that. He looked over his shoulder and watched as she walked to her favourite place—the one where she could see without being seen—and remained there even until he'd reached the keep.

Had that kiss affected her as it had him? His cock-stand had not diminished at all and strengthened every time he thought of her or the taste of her mouth. And it continued for more time than he expected.

As he tried to sleep that night, Robert's words about recognising the weakness that she was echoed in his thoughts and kept him from rest.

Chapter Eleven

She smiled more.

Iain noticed that the next morning. She greeted him at table as the family did and how no one else saw the blush that brought a lovely colour to her cheeks he could not explain. He made it through the meal, discussing with Robert and Struan the plans for the arrival of The Mackintosh and several other chieftains in the coming weeks, before staring at her.

When she reached up and touched her mouth when she thought no one was watching, sliding the tip of her finger along her bottom lip, he remembered the taste and feel of it. She dropped her hand to her lap for the moment had passed. He forced himself and his attention back to Robert's conversation.

His father's twin sister, Arabella, was married to Brodie Mackintosh, who'd claimed his position as chieftain after a bloody and devastating fight against his cousin—and the Camerons, too. That fight began when Brodie was accused, and appeared guilty, of killing Iain's father. Only months later and after many lives were lost, did the truth out, helped along by the only witness to the murder—Alan Cameron, Robert's stepson.

Iain had heard about how his uncle-by-marriage had stood at Alan's and Robert's backs in their fight to defeat the ruthless Gilbert Cameron. And Robert's recent disclosures had given him a better understanding of how it had come to be.

It was that same Mackintosh uncle who had helped Robert find and save Iain when he and Davidh's son were taken by outlaws to be used against the Cameron chieftain. That was when and how he'd met Brodie and his Aunt Arabella. She'd recognised him almost immediately after seeing him for the first time, but had not revealed her knowledge to anyone but his own mother.

So, Brodie Mackintosh and Robert Cameron had been allies for years and they were friends as well. Davidh's son Malcolm, named for Iain's father, had been fostering in Drumlui Keep with Brodie for several years now, learning the skills of a clerk. Iain smiled as he realised that Colm would most likely accompany The Mackintosh here on this visit.

As the impending visit grew closer, Glynnis improved so much. From being almost chairbound and never being far from Lady Elizabeth's side, she fell back into her former duties. Each day saw her brighter and stronger and more at ease—with those around her, with him and even with herself. And more involved with everyone around her.

Iain neither ignored her nor sought her out, but in

a household and keep of this size and nature, they ended up together many times. At meals. In the yard or outbuildings. Riding along the loch. And each encounter, each day he spent time with her, he understood the true weakness she was for him.

As she changed each day, he knew he still loved her. Oh, even before that kiss, he had wanted her. The pain of losing her and the effort it took to move on and claim his life had not diminished his feelings for her. Watching her smile and hearing her laugh warmed his heart even while she remained impossible for him.

As he caught up with her this day as she crossed the yard, she stopped and waited for him.

'Good day to you, Iain.' She carried a basket on her arm and her pace had been brisk until he reached her. 'Are you going to the village?'

'I was not,' he said. 'Are you?' He had no plans, for he'd finished the preparations Robert had assigned him earlier and his only plan was to take a ride to the mill either this day or on the morrow.

'I am seeking your mother.'

'Are you well?' He lifted his hand to shade his eyes from the sun overhead so he could see her more clearly.

'I am. I have these for Coira and thought your mother could take them the next time she or Jeannie go out there.' Glynnis held out the basket and he saw a package wrapped in cloth in it. 'I wanted to thank her for all of her help while I was…staying in the cottage.'

'I would not admit this too close to our kitchens,

but Coira's stews are the best I have ever tasted,' he said, lowering his voice in spite of not caring if he was overheard. James's wife had heard his compliments many, many times. Now it was her turn to laugh and he drank in the sound and joy of it. Iain could not turn his gaze away from her.

'My mother will not be venturing far from the keep or village while The Mackintosh visits. Sheena is coming with Robbie and—' Glynnis might not know about Sheena's condition yet and he should not reveal that news. 'I could take you to the mill, if you like?'

She looked at the basket and at him before nodding. 'I would like that.'

It did not take long for them to get horses and be on their way, out through the village and on the road to the mill. He guided his mount to an easy pace and she rode at his side. As they passed the turning place in the road, the one leading off to the cottage, Glynnis shifted her gaze in that direction before riding on.

'I am not the same woman who stayed at the cottage.' Unsure if she would say more, he waited. 'I was so lost when I arrived here.'

'Your stay there and at the keep now seems a success.' Iain eased the reins back in his hands to slow his horse's gait to an even walk. 'Have you found what you were seeking?'

'A respite. A chance to recover before returning to my father's house. Lady Elizabeth was gracious in spite of the risks she took in arranging it.' At his raised eyebrow, she smiled. 'Oh, Robert told me himself of his opposition to it,' Glynnis said. 'Well, when he discovered my presence and that you had discovered me.'

'Glynnis, Robert—'

'All is well, Iain,' she interrupted him. 'He explained his reasons and they made sense. He is chieftain and must see to the priorities of his clan before anything else. I understand.'

''Twas about us,' he admitted. It was clear that they were the only two who had not discussed the awkward situation.

'Aye.' She met his gaze. 'And, as I explained to him, there is no "us" and we are simply old friends meeting once more.'

As he stared at her mouth, remembering *that* kiss, it was hard to convince himself of that. The blush rising in her fair cheeks revealed she was remembering it, too. The attraction and pleasure in that caress of her mouth that remained in his memories made it hard to believe it was between old friends.

'Ah, the kiss,' she whispered. 'Had you not been curious, Iain? Had you not wanted to see if our memories matched the truth of it?'

'The truth of it?'

'The feelings of youth. The kisses we shared those years ago.'

'That kiss was nothing like I remembered.' Even now, his body reacted in a way it never had with her before when he was that younger man to whom she referred.

'In some ways, it could not be. We are different from the naive, young people who believed that love could be enough.' A layer of resignation flowed through her words. 'I just needed to know if…'

'If?' He held his horse steady beneath him, waiting on her words. She shrugged and gave him a sad smile.

'It matters not now,' she said. Staring off down the road, she adjusted the way she sat and shook her reins, urging her horse to move.

She did not ride hard, but she kept the horse's pace fast enough that they could not speak as they rode. When they came to the mill and the nearby miller's house, Glynnis gave no sign of being worried about anything. A smile close to the gracious ones she was known for now lay on her face as James walked to them. His son took hold of her horse and helped her down as Iain slid off his.

James directed her to Coira in their cottage and Iain remained there to talk with the miller about the repairs and how the new timbers had settled in over the weeks since being placed. Glynnis reached the open door and knocked on the frame of it, but before she entered, there was a moment when she paused. He watched as she closed her eyes briefly and leaned her head down before she stepped within.

As though she was preparing for something challenging. Girding her loins for some battle within? All he could think on as she crossed the threshold was her unasked question.

What had she needed to know?

If what?

It would hurt, she knew that when she'd planned the gift and made the decision to bring it here herself.

The last time she was in Coira and James's cottage, their bairn was not. Or she was napping in the other chamber. Either way, Glynnis had not been forced to see one so young. Though she'd seen others' weeuns in the village and even in the keep, it did not hurt as much now as it had the first time she'd encountered children. But she took a moment to prepare herself before entering the always bustling cottage. Chances were wee Allee would be here. And as she suspected, Coira was sat by the hearth, with her youngest bairn at her breast, stirring a pot of some stew or soup that smelled delicious.

Impossibly, her own breasts tingled as she heard the sound of the bairn suckling at her mother's. But she'd never had the chance. She swallowed against the tightness in her throat as Coira greeted her.

'My lady, come ye in.' Coira stood and waved for Glynnis to take a seat at the table. 'Do ye wish some water or I could—'

'Nay, Coira. Do not interrupt what you are doing there.' As her mother moved, the bairn released her hold and gave Glynnis a milky smile.

'Ah, she was done, my lady,' Coira said, as she tucked her blouse back in place and tugged the end of her plaid over her shoulder.' She put the bairn down and the little lass wobbled away, chasing a ball into a corner. 'Are ye sure ye dinna want something to drink?'

Glynnis put the basket on the table as she sat down. 'Only if you are getting something for yourself, Coira. I did not wish to make work for you.'

Coira crossed the cottage with an efficiency of

movement, never wasting a step or an open hand. Soon, she'd poured two cups of ale and joined Glynnis, scooping up her daughter as she did. As she watched, the woman untied the lass's braids, ran her fingers through her hair and retied them.

'What brings ye out here?' Coira asked. After setting the girl back on her feet, she drank deeply of the cup.

'I brought these,' Glynnis said, easing the basket across the table to her. 'As a way to thank you for your many kindnesses, Coira. I ken the lady asked you to do it, but you helped me when I needed it most and I will always be grateful.'

Glynnis remembered little from that day, but the memories of the waves of ungodly pain remained with her. And, as she offered a quick prayer up to the Almighty, she was glad that that had not happened again since. Coira reached over slowly and patted Glynnis's hand before lifting the wrapped bundle from the basket and tugging the string free of it.

'Oh, my lady! These are so lovely. And so thoughtful of ye. My thanks.' Coira took each one out and exclaimed over them—about the fine stitching or the colour or the soft fabric Glynnis had found at Achnacarry to make them from. But the grief that was never far away must have shown in her eyes when Coira met her gaze. 'So ye hiv lost a bairn?'

Glynnis could only whisper the word. 'Aye.'

''Tis the way of things, my lady. Far too many are lost too early. My James and I hiv lost three.' Coira rose. 'But we hiv been blessed with our five.' Coira moved her hand in the sign of the Cross and turned to fetch the pitcher. 'Ye are young, my lady. There is still more time for ye.'

There would never be children for her. All the midwives and healers consulted had agreed. The last pregnancy had damaged her too much to get pregnant again. Glynnis would never carry a bairn.

At some noise, she looked up and saw Iain watching her from the doorway. His gaze was a knowing one, for he'd heard at least part of their conversation, and she could not tolerate it. Blinking several times, she smiled at Coira.

'I am glad you like them.'

'Iain, did ye ken what Lady Glynnis made for wee Alice?' Coira asked as she spotted him, too. Holding up one of the garments so he could see it, she smiled. 'Such lovely work.'

He walked towards them, followed by the miller, and made some comments that she did not hear. James waited for Coira to show him each piece she'd made before turning to thank her. He lifted Alice into his arms and carried her closer as he did so.

''Tweren't expecting such a gift, my lady,' he said. 'We thank ye.'

Without warning, the bairn lunged forward out of his arms towards her and Glynnis could only catch the bairn to keep her from falling. Alice laughed as bairns her age did, so pleased with herself, and Glynnis searched deep within for all her control to withstand the irresistible urge to wrap the lass up in her arms and never let her go. But the little one broke the spell by turning back to her father and lurching now in his direction.

'She wi' do this for hours if we let her, my lady,' James said in a voice filled with love and pride. 'Here now, wee lassie, go to yer mam.'

Coira took hold of Alice and the bairn seemed to accept her game was over. It was all Glynnis could do not to snatch the child back. This was not her child. Her empty womb and arms would always be just that. Her racing heart would not calm nor would her irrational need to hold that little one again. Until he spoke, she'd forgotten Iain was there.

'Lady? Do not forget that Lady Elizabeth waits on your return.'

Lady Elizabeth? She'd made no such arrangements. Glynnis turned to Iain and saw the lie on his face.

He knew.

He knew she suffered and he was giving her a way out.

'I had forgotten,' she said to the couple. 'We must return to Achnacarry.'

'We willna keep ye from yer duties,' James said.

'Thank ye, my lady,' Coira said. Glynnis had made it through the door when Coira called out to her, 'Yer basket.'

The need to flee before breaking into pieces was so strong she could not bring words to mind.

'Worry not, Coira,' Iain said as he guided her to her horse. 'Send it to the keep when next you come into the village.'

Glynnis's hands shook as he handed her up and he must have noticed, for once he was mounted, he took hold of her reins and led her…somewhere. She could not remember leaving the mill or where they went.

The next thing she knew she was standing in that cottage in the forest, her refuge, and he was watching her.

Waiting.

For words that would not come.

'Glynnis,' he said softly. 'You lost a babe.'

It was not a question. He knew.

And now her shame would be complete and her failure would be exposed. And Iain would never look at her so kindly when the truth was out.

How had he never seen it or suspected it before? He lost all his abilities to think clearly if it involved Lady Glynnis MacLachlan. One of the skills he'd strengthened over these last years was to coldly evaluate a situation and assess what must be done. Now? She had returned and he was…unable. Robert's words echoed in his thoughts and Iain's confidence in knowing his strengths and weaknesses diminished.

The desolation in her eyes when she watched Alice and when the lass jumped into her arms was as clear as the loch on a summer's day. But he had heard Coira's question, and Glynnis's devastating simple response forced him to recognise the truth.

Glynnis had not come here only because of losing her husband, she'd come here to grieve the loss of her child.

As he watched, she'd begun to lose control, something she would be horrified to do. So, he made up an excuse and got her out before she could. He thought distance would improve her condition, but she stood here in the centre of the cottage, unable to speak or even be aware of herself.

'Glynnis?' The bleak expression did not change. He reached inside his sporran and took out his flask. Filled with the chieftain's best, it could help her get over this shock. 'Take a drink of this.'

When she did not move, he lifted it to her lips and tilted it until the golden liquid trickled into her mouth. About to reach up to ease her head back, he felt her pull on the flask, taking a mouthful and then another one. After she swallowed again, he lifted it from her lips. Her eyes fluttered and her body wobbled, giving him little warning when she toppled.

Iain caught her and lifted her in his arms, carrying her to the pallet by the wall. He did not want her lying down flat so he sat against the wall and drew her back on his lap. She had not spoken a word yet and Iain was not certain if she would say something or if the emotions within her would just explode out like a festering wound that is lanced.

Holding her in his embrace in silence for some time, he listened to her shallow breaths. Soon, it began to rain outside and the sound of it on the thin roof above them beat a slow rhythm, one he hoped helped calm her. After some time passed and although he expected tears, she eased back and moved over to sit beside him on the pallet. When he took hold of her hand, she allowed it.

'I was carrying when Martainn died. I lost them both,' she whispered. Another breath inhaled and let out. 'I did not wish you to ken I cannot have children.'

The weight of the words and that truth were the

cause for the desolation and the grief in her gaze. The way she lay against him spoke of her defeat and resignation.

'Did you think I would think less of you because of that tragedy?' He shook his head and bumped her shoulder with his, trying to ease the tension between them. 'You think so little of me that you believe me capable of such cruelty?'

'Not cruelty,' she explained. ''Tis the way things are done, the way blame is assigned.'

'Must there be blame, Glynnis? Is the loss not punishment enough?' He'd watched as his mother lost the bairn she carried just after she married Davidh and understood the suffering of body and soul that followed.

'Would that every man believed what you believe, Iain.'

'I am sorry for your terrible losses.' He lifted their joined hands and kissed the back of hers. 'When you left, in spite of…how we ended, I wished nothing but happiness for you. I'd hoped that if you could not marry me, that your marriage would be a good one for you.'

'It was as I—' She shook her head and shrugged. ''Twas not a bad marriage.'

She lapsed into silence and whether due to her reluctance to speak about marrying another man and leaving him behind or due to grief, he did not push her for more.

'What will you do now?' he asked. 'Are you ready to…?' He really had no idea what would happen next to her. All Lady Elizabeth had said was she was here to recuperate. 'Return home?' She'd lived most of her life away from her father's house—did she consider that place home now?

'I wait on my father's call,' she said. Releasing his hand, she climbed to her feet and smoothed her hands down her gown. 'I thought I was ready. I thought I could…' She shrugged and looked at him. 'I could move on.'

'Is there no other choice for you?'

If, when, she returned to her father's control, as a widow with no ties to her husband's family, he would once more plan an advantageous match for her. Though a woman who could not bear a man heirs was looked upon differently from a young and presumed fertile one. Widowers with their own children who needed tending. Second or third sons with no hope of inheriting.

'We both understand the rules under which we live, Iain. And now that you ken the truth of my…' She paused and walked to the doorway, apparently just noticing it was open. 'I have no other choices.'

Then, she altered before his eyes—from defeated to resolved—as he watched her pull her shattered control back into place. Anger built inside him—at her father, her dead husband, at everyone, at himself—that she needs must do that to protect herself. She would never be angry on her own behalf, but it coursed through his blood now. It must have shown for her gaze narrowed.

'I do feel better, Iain. Truly, I am stronger. With each day, I regain myself.'

'Glynnis, I wish—'

'No, Iain, please do not.' She faced him and he was

surprised that the smile on her face was genuine. 'I will wish you well when I go.'

Iain walked to her side and took her hand. She'd stopped him from saying something they could not walk away from. But she would not stop him from saying what he wanted.

'I want you will take the time left to you here and enjoy what you can, Glynnis. Lady Elizabeth was right to offer you a place here.'

'Was she?'

'Aye. I am glad she could help you in your time of need.' He took a step closer and leaned down to touch his mouth to hers. At the last moment, he did not. She did not need the added burden of his attraction to her. 'Come, if you are well, we should return.'

The ride back was accomplished in silence. Iain suspected that Glynnis might not wish to talk when she so clearly needed to regain herself.

As the unchallenged quiet ride revealed, he'd been correct and she'd made no attempts to speak to him until she bade him farewell at the stables and walked off. He was too angry, too filled with a growing rage, to simply attend to the tasks awaiting him.

Iain walked to the training yard and called out challenges to some of the men he noticed there. He needed the fight to burn this fury from his soul.

And fight he did.

Chapter Twelve

M ud dripped into his eyes and mixed with the blood trickling down from the gash on his head and still he fought on. Struggling to his feet, he asked no quarter and gave none in return. Iain did not fear dying—that was not at stake here and now as it would be in a true battle. Kneeling in the muddy puddle, he pulled in deep gasps to fill his chest.

Nay, this was a fight he simply needed to fight. He needed to clear the ire from his veins and to push the overwhelming need to do something truly stupid back down into his control. Before he did something foolish and unforgivable.

He took on all comers, anyone in the yard or who came at hearing the cheering and calls. Anyone. He'd lost count after the first seven. Some of them were easy defeats. Some of them were not quite as predictable. But the one who could put him down and end this madness and rage stood before him now.

Davidh looked on him with knowing eyes as he waited for Iain to climb to his feet. Iain could not meet his stepfather's gaze long, so he stood and shook the mud from his quarterstaff and his hands. He pushed his hair back out of his face and spat out the mouthful he'd sucked in when he hit the dirt.

No matter that his ribs burned from Dearg's well-placed hit and that Simon's slashing blow cut his arm and the blood soaked his shirt before he pulled it off. They'd never bested him before and probably never would.

But Davidh was another matter.

From the smug look on the man's face as Iain readied for his attack, this would not end well. Even knowing that, he could not stop himself from accepting the fight.

The fury had expanded inside him until he could feel it pushing its way out and through. With each yard they covered, he wanted to let it out. But he was with the only one not responsible for the situation. Not truly. Not her fault either. And she was the one who could do the least to change it.

Davidh had waited until Iain was lost in his thoughts and charged across the few paces separating them. Damn the man, but he knew Iain's vulnerabilities in fighting. He took two vicious hits on his back and shoulder as he turned to get better positioned and more balanced. Too late to do him any good, because his stepfather turned into the relentless warrior he was known to be. The half-score and three years between them did not give Iain any advantage. Add his inexperience into the situation and he was damned.

'Have you forgotten how to defend yourself, Iain?'

Davidh taunted as he slammed the wooden weapon several times quickly against Iain's and sent shards of pain up his arms into his shoulders. Mayhap earlier, he would have stood a chance, but now? Not now. 'Twas his own fault for carrying on with this.

Not ready to give up, he crouched and swept his staff out, aiming for Davidh's feet, trying to unbalance him. The blood in his eyes caused him to misjudge the distance between the two of them and Iain was the one to fall. He landed hard on his back, his breath whooshing out of his chest and the edges of his vision constricting. He heard his head hit and felt the blinding pain, then the rest of his world went black.

Glynnis heard the cheering and calling out as soon as it began. Walking from the stables and planning to seek out Lady Elizabeth, she was instead drawn to the spectacle in the training yard. After his infinite kindness to her, something had happened. She saw the fierceness filling Iain's gaze in their last moments together in the cottage and could feel the heat of anger pouring from him in waves. Their ride back was a stilted silence and several times she thought him ready to say something, only to find him looking away.

Yet, by his manners, he was not angry with her. She could not identify the target or reasons for it. So, they left the cottage after she'd gathered herself back together and reminded herself that there was no way to escape encounters with children for the rest of her life.

As they rode back to Achnacarry, the truth that

there was a real and looming possibility that she would marry a man who had children that needed a woman's, a wife's, care struck her. She would not have the choice to turn away if it upset her as she'd done at Coira's. So, she'd decided she must work to bear up when faced with the wee ones. She could not let those emotions defeat her and hold her future prisoner.

Walking back to the fence around the large empty area where the men trained with weapons, she found an opening and edged into it to watch whatever, who- ever, was catching the attention of everyone.

Iain.

Her breath caught in her chest at the sight of him.

He was naked from the waist up, and as had hap- pened at the mill, she could not tear her gaze away. Splattered in the mud of the yard, he bled from sev- eral places and yet it was not his appearance that distressed her. Indeed, none of the other women she now noticed watching seemed bothered by it at all. The mud-encrusted breeches he wore moulded to his powerfully muscled thighs and she could see every movement as he fought one opponent and another and another.

She was so intent on him she could not remem- ber how many he'd fought. When he landed in the mud, bleeding and struggling to breathe, she clutched the wooden fence to keep from falling over. But a hushed silence fell over all those watching as one man strode towards Iain as he yet knelt in the muck. The Cameron's commander, one of the most experi- enced warriors in the entire clan, held the same long wooden weapon in his grip that Iain did as he made his way closer.

As Davidh stood at the ready, Iain pushed to his feet and shifted back and forth, as he pushed his hair away from his face. Glynnis fought not to let the scream building in her out. Glancing around, she saw that she was not the only one caught up in the tension and anticipation. This would bring an end to whatever they were witnessing. Iain had fought as though a berserker of legend, a mindless warrior fighting until there was no possibility of fighting any longer. The anger she'd seen in his gaze had transformed into fury and that had fuelled these battles.

Davidh said something that made Iain pause. Had he called a halt to the fighting? The crowd surged closer to the fence as if they knew what was coming. Did they?

They did.

The commander attacked without warning and she winced as he struck quickly, knocking Iain down and using his movements and weight against him. Fighting the urge to call out to Iain and warn him, Glynnis closed her eyes as the crowd began screaming around her. She only caught the final moment as Iain fell with his head hitting the ground hard as he landed. When he did not move, she did, pushing around those nearest her and through the gate nearby.

If anyone thought it strange that she was the first one to reach his side, they did not say it or stop her. She knelt down and leaned in, calling his name as she eased his head up on her lap.

'Iain? Are you well?' Not waiting for a reply, she

smoothed his hair out of his eyes and wiped the blood and mud away. 'Iain,' she whispered close to his ear. 'You must wake now.'

She slid her fingers through his hair, feeling along his head for the source of the blood. Instead, she felt a lump growing in size on the back.

'My lady, is he awake?' Davidh tossed his weapon aside to a waiting man as he crouched next to them. Before she could answer, he called out to someone nearby, 'Seek out my wife and bring her here.' He looked at someone else. 'The bucket.'

'He still sleeps, Sir Davidh,' she said. Placing her fingers near the bump, she nodded. 'This is swelling quickly.'

'His mother will not be happy if I have harmed him.'

'Did you do it a-purpose?'

He started at her question. 'I did not want to knock him out.' The commander began to say something else and stopped.

'Go on.'

'I wanted to knock some sense into him.' Davidh sighed and touched Iain's cheek. 'It is his weakness, you ken? He thinks too much at times and at others he does not use the wits he was born with.'

'I thought I was your weakness,' she whispered so only Iain would hear her words. It was one of the things that Robert had repeated in their awkward conversation about her and Iain. The chieftain had been trying to be candid, not hurtful. Davidh gained her attention when he cleared his throat. Looking up at the man who'd taken over Iain's training and care, she recognised another knowing gaze.

'I will not be,' she said. Clearing her own tightening throat, she repeated the words to Davidh as though she needed someone to hear her promise. 'I will not be his weakness.'

The bucket was placed at her side, and after easing out from under him, she used the rag in it to clean most of his face. Davidh called out a few more orders that sent those yet lingering about and watching to go. Barely had most moved away when two things happened at the same time.

Iain roused and opened his eyes just as his mother arrived.

'I am well,' he insisted as he tried to sit up. Anna pushed him back down, and though he could have done as he wished, he acquiesced.

Glynnis watched Anna work, healer first, as she assessed the man before the mother questioned her son…and her husband. The easy back and forth of their conversation and the banter in it spoke of a closeness that made Glynnis jealous. Another new emotion she'd not felt for a long time filled her. Though Anna did not dote on her son, her concern was out before everyone. And it made her own heart ache for such a family as they had.

While Anna poked and prodded along his face and head, Iain stared at Glynnis.

'I must be far worse than I thought, for I do not remember fighting you.'

Though his words were spoken as a tease, all she did was burst into tears. Not sad tears. Ones of relief that he was well enough to be able to jest about his condition. Relief that he was awake after such a head injury. Relief. She climbed to her feet with Davidh's help and Iain stood, too.

'I am just glad you aren't badly injured,' she said. 'That is all.'

'He needs to wash so I can stitch the tear on his scalp that is bleeding,' Anna said. The healer gathered up the bloodied rags she'd used and tossed them in the bucket. Picking it up, she nodded at Glynnis. 'You should get Maggie to see to that before the stains set.'

Glynnis glanced down to find the front of her gown was now a messy mix of blood and mud. Instead of the horror she would have felt in earlier days, she was simply glad she'd been there to render him aid until Anna arrived. Taking her leave of the three, she heard Anna order Iain to get washed and see her in the keep for some stitching. One last glance over her shoulder as she left the fenced enclosure revealed Anna and her husband both watching her leave.

For a moment, she'd thought him dead or, at the least, seriously wounded. And she'd reacted without consideration of the correct thing she should do. Oh, she knew that people here thought of her as the perfect noble lady, never stepping outside her designated role or outside the bounds of what was expected of her.

For Iain, she'd thrown all that away without another thought.

Glynnis stumbled over a non-existent obstacle on the ground when the truth struck her.

For Iain, she would throw it all away.

If given the chance.

Glynnis made her way inside and tried to turn her attentions to the preparations underway.

The story of Iain's defeat by his stepfather spread, with some telling the full story of those Iain vanquished. By the time they all gathered for supper, Iain seemed able to laugh at most of the tales told, even adding his own commentary about his prowess and insults about Davidh's age and his other opponents.

He wore his long hair pulled back and she could see where Anna had stitched the skin along his forehead at his hairline. Not the worst wound she'd seen, but it had bled profusely and added to his defeat by blocking his vision. Davidh had hit him on the back and shoulder and his arm had been slashed by another man, but that damage was hidden under his clothes.

Under his clothes.

She'd seen men unclothed before. She'd watched others fight and train, both here and in The Campbell's holdings. But seeing the changes that only three years had wrought in him as he'd fought had taken her breath away. Glynnis also knew she was not the only one who noticed his pleasing form. His muscles. His height. His strength. Even now, she saw some of the women who'd been watching him fight. She'd heard their sighs and had seen them pointing and ogling his naked chest and the rippling contours of his abdomen.

Much as she had wanted to do. But she was a lady and they were serving maids and seamstresses and the like. Women who would see to a man's needs with little care for their reputations. Thinking on it now, Glynnis realised she'd stared without shame at him as he fought. And the desire to touch him had filled her…and now as she watched him speaking and laughing with a few of the men he'd grown up with here at Achnacarry.

What would it be like to touch him? Would he stand still and allow her to explore all the interesting places on his body? Would he guide her fingers to the places he liked to have touched and caressed? Would he—

'You look flushed, Glynnis,' Lady Elizabeth said, motioning for a serving maid to fill Glynnis's cup. 'I hope you are not coming down with fever?' The back of the lady's hand was cool against her cheek as Elizabeth tested it.

'Nay, my lady. I am well.' She took the cup up and swallowed a mouthful of the ale. Her mouth had gone dry at the thoughts she was having about Iain and the ale refreshed her.

'Robbie sent word that he and Sheena will arrive in the morning and I wanted you to ken.'

'We exchanged letters for a while,' she explained. 'But then…'

Lady Elizabeth reached out and patted her hand. 'Many things changed in the last months. Worry not. 'Twill be good for you two to spend some time together.'

She liked Sheena—even though Sheena had stepped into the betrothal meant for Glynnis, it worked out for the best. The youngest daughter of the man called The Beast of The Highlands was quite different from what Glynnis had expected after Robbie's stories. He and

Sheena had become enemies as children and many secrets threatened to ruin any chance they'd had of happiness. Glynnis had protected more than one of Sheena's secrets and they'd become friends.

'I look forward to seeing her,' she said.

From a few comments Robbie had made and from something Iain had said, mayhap without realising it, Glynnis suspected Sheena was carrying. Lady Elizabeth would avoid speaking of it unless necessary, but now, Glynnis found she could not allow her own loss to belittle the joy of her friend. No matter that it would hurt. No matter that it would hurt for some time.

'And I welcome her news,' Glynnis whispered while leaning closer. Elizabeth's eyes widened at the disclosure. 'I promise to let Sheena tell me and will not reveal the truth of how Robbie gave too many hints on his visit.'

'I ken what a struggle it will be for you, Glynnis. The pain of your loss will not retreat quickly. But grief does change and become bearable. It does. I will keep you in my prayers.'

Sheena's arrival in the morn and Glynnis's knowledge of her condition was made less about Glynnis's own reaction when her friend promptly lost the contents of her stomach as soon as her feet touched the ground. Glynnis found herself in the middle of a small group of women who spirited Sheena away to the solar as she recovered from what she called her daily unfortunate act.

Their visit was actually quite pleasant from that time on, for they had much to talk about and the time passed quickly. The Mackintosh and his wife, and their entourage, arrived and many sessions were held among the men, leaving the women on their own for much of the days.

Four days later, on the last day of meetings and discussions, a ceilidh was planned and much work was put into arranging the meal and the musicians and singers who would entertain after supper. Maggie slipped a small packet in her hand sometime during that day and Glynnis tucked it up in her sleeve. She never even remembered it until she was changed for the celebratory gathering.

'Maggie, what is this?' she asked as she pulled the parchment from inside her sleeve and held it up.

'Oh, my lady, I am sorry. A messenger arrived earlier with that while you were busy with Lady Elizabeth.'

'A messenger?'

Glynnis broke the familiar seal, knowing she could not avoid it, and unfolded the parchment. Her father's bold scrawl at the bottom of it forced her to read the whole of it. He'd not heard back from Lady Cameron so he was sending this directly to her.

That was a surprise.

The words she'd known would come and that she dreaded none the less were all there for her to see. Her time here was done, in spite of any efforts by her godmother to extend it. Any misplaced dreams or desires would remain unsatisfied. She must submit to the life her father had chosen for her.

Maggie waited for her to speak, but Glynnis simply shrugged and folded the parchment up. After dressing, she put it in the small box that travelled with her for such things and followed Maggie below.

She would enjoy this night and not speak of the missive from her father until the morn, after Robbie and Sheena had left for Tor, the Mackintoshes had returned to Glenlui and life here had returned to its usual pace.

But not tonight.

Tonight was hers.

Chapter Thirteen

Something was wrong.

As Iain observed her through the supper that marked the ending of The Mackintosh's visit, it was so obvious to him that he could not imagine why others did not see it.

He'd been seated at the other end of the table next to his aunt's cousin-by-marriage and enjoyed the banter between the man and his wife, a MacKay from the far north of Scotland. He'd spoken at length with his aunt as well as his stepbrother Colm, who did accompany the Mackintoshes on this visit and who sat beside him now. They would all be returning for the betrothal ceremony and to meet his bride when she arrived.

Another glance at Glynnis and he caught the moment when she allowed her guarded expression to drop. Oh, something had happened and he suspected it meant she must leave. When the musicians gathered and the tables were moved to allow for dancing, Iain walked to her end of the table and pulled a stool closer to her.

'Glynnis.' He nodded to those sitting around her. 'Will you dance with me later?'

'Another change since last we met,' she said as she smiled at him.

'I fought it for as long as possible,' he admitted. 'And I can promise to try not to step on your toes, though I cannot promise I won't.'

Glynnis laughed and he was struck dumb by the sound of it. It caught Lady Elizabeth's attention and she looked over.

'My dancing skills, my lady. I'm warning Lady Glynnis.'

'Glynnis, I tried, truly I did. But there is a limit to what skills of good society a lady can teach an uncooperative youth.' Lady Elizabeth leaned down as she spoke. 'Though he is much better now than when he crushed his aunt's toe.'

Iain wiped his hands over his face and laughed.

'Or when he tore the edge of my gown off during a lively attempt,' Sheena added from next to the lady.

'Glynnis, let us just say that you risk much if you dance with Iain,' Tomas added. 'I, however, learned to dance well under my mother's tutelage and would be pleased to dance with you.' Tomas stood and pushed forward, holding out his hand to her. Glynnis looked between the two of them and accepted Tomas's hand. 'Keep a close watch on us, Iain, and I will demonstrate it to you.' Iain laughed as they walked down the steps to where the others gathered.

Tomas was a good man, Robert's youngest son, and the one who Iain thought was the better choice for tanist, if he was being truthful with himself. Tomas always stood ready to serve though he would appear unready to take on that responsibility. He hid his competence and skills well beneath the façade he'd created. The musicians began with a lively dance that sent the dancers circling around the floor, pausing in small groups and moving on. She was radiant, laughing and speaking to Tomas as they moved around the area.

Glynnis laughed at something Tomas said and Iain loved seeing the rising flush of enjoyment in her face. This is what he wanted for her—a life filled with joy, not sorrow. He wished he could see her like this every day. He turned on the stool to see the whole group of those dancing.

He wanted her. He wanted her in his life, in his arms.

In his bed. Because she was already in his heart and soul.

The irony in this situation was not missed. Three years ago he was the one not worthy, not eligible, of someone of her status and position and expectations. She was of noble birth and supposed to marry someone of the same. Her father had held the power and he had…none.

Because of that rejection, he had changed himself, his life and *his* expectations. He became the one with choices. Raised up, about to be titled and married to someone connected to royal blood, he was the one with the power to say aye or nay. If he'd harboured a hope deep within that she would be the one, he had never admitted it to himself or anyone else.

But…he had.

In those early months of struggling against what

he felt for her, against his own weaknesses and in-ability and lack of knowledge and skill, he continued to hope it would give him a chance to claim her before it was too late. It was only after hearing of her marriage that his foolish hope crashed and he had to re-examine the reasons for continuing.

Davidh had been the one who spoke of his friend Malcolm Cameron and the hopes they'd had as lads. The high chair of the clan was something that would come to Malcolm and he had to do little to claim it. For Iain, it would not come easy, if at all, and Davidh had inspired him to let go of his past and claim the future that had never been his father's.

As he watched Glynnis spin in Tomas's grasp, he remembered the exact moment he'd given up on her. On them.

From then on, he'd never looked back. Never doubted. Only moved forward, towards his goal.

And now, he only had to reach out and take it. Well, take the opportunity, marry the woman, make the alliance and continue preparing for the time he would be called to lead.

As though taunting him, cheers rang out as the music stopped and those dancing clapped at the end of it. He searched for Glynnis and found her standing with a different partner. She smiled at him and shrugged as the music began anew, drawing her and her partner into those gathered.

'She has recovered more than I dared hope she would,' Lady Elizabeth said softly. He turned and found her at his side, watching the dancing. 'The pieces are mended.'

'Are they, lady?' He studied her face for some sign of deception or misunderstanding.

'As much as they can be. Not everything is within our control, Iain. Even you must ken that?'

'Och, aye, I have learned that the hard way, my lady.' He glanced back to see Glynnis laughing once more and his heart warmed. 'Has there been word yet?'

Elizabeth did not pretend to misunderstand. She moved her gaze from him to Glynnis and studied her. 'Not to me.'

'I think he has contacted Glynnis.'

Elizabeth's gaze narrowed and she let out a sad sigh. 'And what will you do?'

'For all the reasons you ken about and mostly to not cause her any more pain, I will stand and watch her leave…again.'

But now, this night, she was here and he would be with her. He stood and excused himself, striding quickly to the dancing and waiting for the current one to slow. He wasted not another moment, nor took the chance that someone else would claim her hand for the next dance. Iain approached directly and held out his hand to her. A few groans of disappointment from other men who'd had the same idea echoed around them.

Glynnis looked neither left nor right, but only at him, as she took the hand he offered. Iain tugged her closer and they took their place among the others.

'I must defend my reputation, Glynnis. Tell me true—did Tomas injure your toes?' he teased her as they waited for the music to start. The piper and bodhran player paused to quench their thirst, but he did not release her.

'Tomas was skilled at dancing, Iain.' She said it giving no indication of whether she was jesting or speaking the truth. The drummer tapped a beat on his leather bodhran and she tapped her foot to it. 'I am willing to give you a chance to show me if you can best him.'

Iain leaned his head back and laughed before leading her into the first round of steps. This song picked up speed and he could only watch her and count his steps as they circled the other couples into the centre, out to the edge and back again. He let go of tomorrow and simply enjoyed the touch of her hand, the sound of her laughter and the smile she gifted to him.

The first dance ended and he held her hand, not letting go of her. His narrowed gaze and challenging glare told any approaching man that he should stand down—he would not be turning her over to another. After several more, he guided her to an alcove, grabbing two cups from a servant's tray as they walked together.

'Where is Tomas?' she asked, searching the chamber for the man. 'I must tell him you did better than I expected.'

'Worry not, I will make certain he kens when next I see him.' They laughed again and both drank deeply from their cups. The ale was refreshing and it took but a short time to regain their breath after the strenuous moves of the dances.

'I have something to ask you, Iain,' she said. Her gaze took a serious turn and he waited for the question or request. 'Would you come to your mother's workroom when everyone seeks their rest?' The words were spoken casually, almost uncaring, yet the importance was so clear to him.

'Below-stairs? Have you need of help there?' She'd been working at the lady's side in all the preparations and he wondered if she needed something stored there.

'I do not think you are staying in the chamber you use here in the keep?' He shook his head. 'So, you are planning to leave and sleep in the house in the village?'

'Aye. Too many guests needed sleeping space, so I gave it up to guests.'

'As did I,' she said. 'I have been sleeping in the lady's solar with some of the other unmarried women.' She turned then, facing him, and moved closer to him. Lifting her head, she stared at him. 'So, will you come to your mother's workroom later?'

'Before I leave the keep?'

'Aye.' Colour flooded her cheeks at the word and Iain could not work out the cause of it. But, if she asked for him to go there, he would.

'I will stop there before I go back to the village.'

She stood up on her toes, which he must not have injured, and kissed him quickly on his cheek. She was gone as someone called her name.

And he could think of nothing else the rest of the gathering.

Glynnis waited for most to be leaving the hall and seeking their beds or chambers before making her way down the stairway in the far tower and seeking Anna's workroom. She'd had the chance to explore the chamber while running an errand here for the lady and was pleased to see that it had the supplies she needed.

She turned the last corner and reached it. Easing the latch up and opening the door slowly, she checked to see if anyone was within. Holding her lantern higher, she saw that the room was empty. Was it wrong to feel excited about the coming night? Well, excited even while wondering if Iain would arrive as he'd said he would, and worried that he would throw her invitation in her face.

Glynnis was wagering that the expression in his gaze while he watched her and his recent touches and caresses under the cover of the dances they shared meant he would.

Everything in her upbringing should prevent her from even considering such a night as this one. She was not married any longer and under the control of her father, who would object, her being a widow or not. She knew that many widows, highborn and low, enjoyed more freedom, but what she was asking of Iain felt…sinful.

And it was, or rather it would be, if she had the night she wanted.

Glynnis walked to the small, closeted area in the corner and held the lantern up. A pile of blankets sat on a small stool along with a few pillows. Anna kept them and the small cot that lay tucked under one of the tables, in case she needed to rest while waiting on a concoction or other medicament to cook or cool.

Even now in the warmest weather, these chambers below ground remained chilled, so the blankets would be a blessing. Gathering them up, she carried them to one of the long worktables.

Her stomach tightened and a strange feeling made her nervous as she waited. Glancing around, she saw so many jars and bottles and bowls, some covered, others not, and wished she could identify them. What she needed was something to calm her nerves while she waited. Oh, to have Iain's flask right now.

'I do not have my flask with me, but you're welcome to some of this.'

She spun around to find Iain standing inside the chamber, holding out a small jug of what must be the chieftain's special *uisge beatha* to her. Had she spoken aloud? He smiled and held it out until she crossed the chamber and took it from him.

He was here!

He was here.

Could he see her hands trembled as she took the jug from him? Glynnis turned back to the shelves and tables, looking for some cups. It took longer than it should to find them, even though they sat just inches away from her hands. When she faced him, he was just staring at her with the most intense gaze and she stopped moving. She stopped breathing.

'I ken you do not fear me, so why is your gaze filled with it now?'

'I have something to ask you, Iain. And I ken not what you will say.'

'Then I guess you will just have to ask me to find

out, Glynnis. I doubt I could deny you anything, but what is it you want?'

She inhaled slowly as she tried to gather the words, the right words, together that would explain what she wanted and why. They all flew free in her thoughts and she lost them, as he waited for her to speak.

Finally, when no explanation would come, she just blurted out the simplest one.

'You, Iain. I want you.'

Would he laugh? Was he shocked? From his silence and the way one of his brows lifted, she thought he must be unable to believe she'd said something so outrageous.

Realising she held the cups of powerful spirits in her hands, she lifted one to her lips and tossed it back. The burn as it rolled over her tongue and down her throat cleared her thoughts. As she handed the other to him, she wondered if she had the courage to see this through.

'And I want you, Glynnis. I always have. I never stopped.'

Her whole body ached at his words. A throbbing began deep within her, something dormant that now reawakened. She knew she must explain this wild, unconventional, unladylike, sinful plan of hers before…before he could decide.

'I have received word from my father.'

'You must go home. I thought so,' he said.

'You did?'

'There was something different about you at supper and the celebration. I noticed it. Lady Elizabeth did as well.' He drank down the contents of his cup and held it out to her for more.

Good. It gave her something else to do while proposing this scandalous thing to him. Lifting the jug, she poured more of the amber liquid in both.

'Have a care. That jug has much more than my flask carries.' It did not stop him from drinking it down in one mouthful—as she did herself. That eyebrow raised again. How had she never noticed that before?

'So, aye, I must return and accept whatever arrangements my father has made for my future.' She pulled them back to the matter at hand.

'Must you?'

'Must I? What choice do I have, Iain? I have no skills or other kin to call on for my support. If I defy my father, any of his allies will turn against me and not take me in.' She put the cup down on the table and clasped her hands together. 'No matter, I must return to do his bidding just as you must carry on with your duties here. You chose loyalty and a path and have worked hard for the honours you are receiving and you deserve it all.' Glynnis reached out and touched his hand. 'And that your father would be so proud to see you accomplish it adds to the importance of following it through.'

'What will you do?' he asked, covering her hand with his.

'Marry as I must just as you will.'

'I wish—' She boldly placed her fingers on his lips to stop him.

'We will each do our duty, Iain.' She saw so many regrets in his gaze. 'When we must.'

He lifted her hand from his mouth and tangled their fingers together. 'When we must?'

'On the morrow, I will prepare and leave for my father's lands, where he will marry me off to a man who needs no more children or has some other use for me. But, Iain, I do not want to waste this night and walk away with more regrets.'

'What are you saying, Glynnis?' He pulled her closer and leaned into her. A gentle touch of his mouth stirred such need within her.

'Give me this night with you. I am tired of living with the questions and regrets of my actions three years ago. And in fear of lying with another man who loves me not. If we cannot be together after this, then I want this one night with the man I love to carry with me in my memories.'

She glanced away, afraid of what his immediate reaction would be. A slight squeeze of his fingers brought her gaze back to his.

''Tis yours, Glynnis.'

Chapter Fourteen

He thought he'd come up with every possibility of why Glynnis wanted to meet him here. A final kiss goodbye was the most logical one. But never in his life would he have dreamed she would ask this of him. Still, he could not, in all good conscience, take advantage of a distraught woman or one not able to see all the consequences of such an action.

Especially not Glynnis.

'Are you certain about this?' He slid his hands along her arms to her shoulders, holding her close, already feeling the disappointment that would fill him when she came to her senses over this. 'Is it wise?'

'I am certain. 'Tis not wise,' she said, moving into his arms and leaning her head against his chest. He shifted his hands across her back to hold her there. Iain stroked her hair, pulling it free of the braid she always wore. She lifted her head back and smiled at him—one he was sure every temptress wore when doing their best.

To hold her like this. To kiss her as he'd wanted

to since desire had overwhelmed his reason in the stables when she'd asked for one. To peel off her layers and discover the woman he'd missed for nigh on three years. He wanted all of those things and more.

Her smile faded and she stepped out of his embrace.

'If you do not wish to, I understand, Iain.'

'Not wish to, Glynnis?' He barely had control of himself right now as she stood before him offering herself to him. 'Does this feel like a man who does not want you?'

He took her hand and placed it on his hardened flesh, guiding it along his length—his very erect, very ready flesh. When she closed her fingers around him, he did lose control. He released her hand and encircled her face with his.

'Glynnis,' he whispered. 'Glynnis.'

Iain took her mouth, not a kiss. Nay, he possessed it with his lips and tongue and tasted her deeply. Sweet, with the hint of the *uisge beatha*. Her lips melded to his and he eased her head and kissed her over and over until they were breathless. Her fingers yet surrounded him and she met every stroke of his tongue on hers with a stroke on his cock.

He walked her back several steps until they stopped, her body trapped between one of the worktables and his own body. He noticed when she released him to slide her hands into his hair and keep his mouth against hers.

He needed to touch her, to feel the heat of her skin, the tightness of her core. Lifting her to sit on the table, he stepped between the legs she spread for him as he unlaced the back of her gown and tugged it off her shoulders. Glynnis leaned away, her eyes filled with desire, and watched his every move. Once the gown was out of the way, he untied the ribbon that held her shift and eased it open. Iain reached out to caress the dark pink nipples now exposed to him.

'So beautiful,' he said as he took the left one in his mouth and flicked the edge of his tongue over it.

Glynnis sighed and then gasped with every taste he took and his erection surged between their bodies. He captured her other breast in his hand, sliding his thumb over the taut tip and stroking it until she pressed into his grasp. Her breast filled his grasp, and as he moved to suckle on the other side, she could not stop the sounds of pleasure from erupting. Glynnis arched her body against his, wanting more. Wanting all of him.

'I want to touch you, Glynnis. I want to feel your heat.' He took hold of her gown and waited on her reaction. She held on to his shoulders and nodded. 'Good lass,' he whispered.

He gathered the length of her gown in his hands and pushed the garment up to her hips, allowing him to see her most private place. A wave of nervousness passed through her. This was the first time since… well, since everything and he was the first, only, man other than her husband to see and touch her.

As though he'd heard her self-doubts, he whispered again, 'Steady on now, Glynnis.' He kissed her quickly and waited for her. 'Steady on.' She nodded and with just the tips of his fingers, he caressed the insides of her thighs, seeking out the places that made her sigh and tense. Her breath held, as inch by inch, he touched her until he reached the curls there.

'Iain.' She moaned out his name. So close. So close and yet the anticipation and need for his touch made her shudder.

It took only three strokes of his knuckles through her intimate folds to have her panting in shallow breaths. Her body wept its arousal on to his hand and she began moving against it.

He whispered to her, 'Touch. Me. Glynnis.' He groaned out the words and heat poured through her blood.

She loosened his belt as he rubbed deeper into those folds. Luckily, he'd worn his tunic and trews to supper and she had only two layers of clothing to get through. And she did it quickly, increasing her speed as he did until she opened his trews and took hold of him. Their moans blended and echoed across the chamber.

Glynnis stroked his length, using her fingers to encircle his hardness as Iain moved one hand to her head and brought her mouth to his. He was hard, growing harder in her grasp as she massaged the length of him. She was touching him as she'd wanted and he thrust into her hands, telling her he liked it. From the need spiralling inside her, the tension tightening and her body's wetness at the growing pleasure of his touch, Glynnis wanted the rest. To be filled with him. To join with him.

'Now, Iain. Take me now.'

All of Iain's plans of making love to her in a slow and satisfying way, of bringing her to completion with a building pleasure, disappeared at her words. He guided her hips just over the edge of the table, wrapped his arm around her waist and thrust into her, deep and hard and fast.

Everything stopped. He watched her face as he filled her and withdrew almost all the way out. Her teeth worried the edge of her lower lip, but the smile returned as he plunged once again. He paused, buried within her, and eased her knees up and around his hips before repeating the movement. A wonderful moan escaped her as he continued. She put her hands on the table behind her to brace herself against his thrusts.

Iain looked at her and fell in love again.

Her hair was loose and wild around her face and flowing over her shoulders. Her shift gaped open, allowing him to see her perfect breasts, tipped in tight, dark pink nipples that made his mouth water. Her head fell back and a low whimper began deep in her throat as the muscles within her tightened around his flesh. Rippling waves that urged him to his own release. And his body did—spirals of pleasure burst through him as his seed spilled. Her woman's flesh trembled until she, too, arched in passion against him and he absorbed the keening sound by kissing her.

He did not know how much time had passed before they came back to themselves, but he felt her shiver as gooseflesh rose on her skin. Shifting her back to sit on the table, he tugged his trews back up and shook out the length of her gown to cover her bare legs. Iain could not help but stare at her dishevelled loveliness which made him laugh. It got her attention.

'I fear I should beg your pardon, for I treated you less like the noblewoman you are and more like a round-heeled serving maid sneaking off with her lover,' he said as he continued to right her garments and help her down to stand. ''Twas not how I pictured this happening between us.'

''Twas how I'd hoped it would be.' This was spoken quietly as she gathered her hair back over her shoulders and he looked at her to see if she was jesting.

'I realised weeks ago that I wanted this. Wanted you. And whene'er I imagined it, I wanted you to take my breath away.'

He laughed at her honesty and her composure. Tupping Lady Glynnis MacLachlan on a table in a workroom was not something he would have ever considered a possibility. And that she had been considering it for weeks made him want to laugh aloud. But having taken her quickly, and thoroughly from the look of her, he thought he might like to do it again.

His way.

Slowly.

On warm blankets.

Naked, skin against skin.

And again.

'Aye,' she said. He blinked and frowned, for he'd not asked a question. 'Aye, I want to have you again,' she admitted.

He felt the heat fill his face and was not certain if it was a blush to match the one in her cheeks or just desire rising.

'Then have me, my lady. I do your bidding this night.'

* * *

The second time was not as slow as he'd wished. One moment he was teasing her breasts with his teeth and the next, she managed to roll them both until she straddled him and controlled their movements. Oh, he could have rolled back easily and taken the lead, but when he could have the lovely Glynnis astride him, with her beautiful breasts that perfectly filled his hand or in his mouth so close above him, why would he?

There was an instant, as she rode him, when he felt like this was nothing but a dream. One he'd had so many times since he realised he loved her and could never keep her. He'd been so young that his idea of how they would be together was so innocent. Not until he'd found a willing village widow had he any idea of the extent or imaginative ways of bed play. The reality of it with Glynnis this night far surpassed any of his experiences or those naive dreams and now these memories would remain.

He could not miss the hint of desperation that entered her gaze when she did not think he was watching. It was as she'd said—she was trying to savour as much pleasure in this night as she could.

All the while preparing herself to accept the life she could not change.

And never once did she beg him to fight for her or to ask her father to change his mind on the matter. Nor did she suggest anything else but that they were duty-bound and nothing should change that. He could hear the fates laughing at him now. Now that he was within weeks of the final step that would see him attain everything he'd wanted. Now that she was the one taken out of contention, out of his possible choices, because she had proven unacceptable.

Not in his eyes. Never in his. Yet the rules of hierarchy and inheritance and the men who controlled such matters did not favour a woman unable to bear children. As she could not.

Understanding the difficult decision she'd made between them the last time and that it was now his for the same reasons, he would give her what she'd asked him for and do everything he could to make it easier for her to leave this time than he had the first time.

So, if he accepted this noble decision of his and understood all the reasons for it, why did he feel he was making the wrong choice?

The third time that night was the one he'd wanted—gentle, caressing, teasing, pleasuring, filled with sighs and moans as he savoured every touch and taste of her. The fourth began as an exploration of each other and ended in a silent, slow-building explosion of bliss as they joined their bodies.

But, even worn out from their explosive passion, the question that had plagued him earlier followed into his dreams as he drifted to sleep between their bouts of lovemaking. He feared it would haunt him for the rest of his life—the life he'd chosen.

What if he'd been wrong?

Glynnis shifted against the warmth at her back and felt the twinges and aches as she turned over to face Iain. He yet slept—well, dozed—and so she lay watching him. The sounds and subtle changes as the household woke to begin their day could be heard if one knew what to listen for, as she did.

They did not have much time.

Glynnis studied his face, every curve, every angle, so that she would remember this Iain. At ease. Satiated. Well pleasured.

Kind. Giving. Considerate.

The tears formed and trickled down her cheeks. She'd sworn that she could handle this with some dignity and she would. This night had been perfect, exactly what she'd imagined and wanted and needed, and she would not ruin it with tears. Dashing them away, she lay in the warm cocoon they'd made with the blankets and pillows, gathering her resolve around her once more. Finally, as the pale light of day teased its arrival through the small window in the wall that looked out on the yard, Glynnis knew she must leave.

They must part.

'Dinna greet, lass.' His gentle touch on her cheeks where the tears had not dried nearly undid her.

''Tis time, Iain. The kitchen servants will be about their chores and we cannot be seen leaving here together.'

Taking a deep breath to strengthen her will, she started to turn away from him. He would not allow her to move away. He trapped her with his arm around her body and pulled her back to him.

'A proper farewell then?' he asked. If she gave any sign she wanted to leave his embrace now, he would let her go.

'I would make this our final farewell, Iain. 'Twill be difficult enough pretending before everyone that I am happy to leave, but seeing you will…' She did not finish. She did not need to, for he understood. Kissing the tears from her cheeks, he wrapped her in his arms and whispered her name.

Glynnis opened to his kiss and allowed his touch. Though more soothing or caring than arousing, she enjoyed every second of it since it would have to last a very long time in her memories. When it was done, when they were done, he pressed his lips to her forehead in a silent kiss.

He released her and climbed to his feet, before helping her to stand. They moved around each other in a slow, silent, sad dance as they dressed and readied themselves to leave this time out of time behind. Soon, tucked and sorted, dressed and braided with the workroom returned to its usual condition, they stood at the door without moving. Glynnis leaned into him for one last time before lifting the latch.

They decided that Iain would leave first, going out to the yard through the door at the far end of the corridor so it would appear to anyone in the keep that he returned from his mother's house in the village. As she waited, listening to his footsteps for as long as she could hear them, Glynnis was glad she'd done this.

Making her way up the stairs and to the lady's solar, she'd only just undressed and lain down on the pallet assigned to her when the first maid came in to set the fire and another to bring fresh water for washing. Try as she might, she could not fall asleep in the short while before Maggie arrived to help her dress.

The day was a busy one, with most of their visitors departing and the work to put things back aright after so many adjustments to chambers and beds. Once the last party rode out through the gates, Glynnis handed the letter from her father to Lady Elizabeth.

'So, Iain was correct?'

'About what, my lady?'

'He was watching you dance and said he thought your father might have contacted you.' Her god-mother reached out and took hold of her hand. 'Did you enjoy last night, Glynnis?'

'My lady?' she asked, startled by such an unexpected question. Had they been seen together after all?

'The dancing. The company. You seemed to be enjoying it all, my dear.'

'I did, Lady Elizabeth. For the first time in such a long time, I did.' Though she meant it about so much more than just dancing, she did not have to reveal the rest. The lady folded the letter into its original packet.

'I hope your father does not blame you for the delay. I just wanted you to return home healed. Well.'

'He seems to be more confused than angry at your lack of response, so I doubt it. And though it may cause you some difficulty with your husband, you should let him ken about it so he is not surprised by any questions my father might ask.'

She understood the tension her arrival and stay here had caused between the lady and her lord and wished no further discord be connected to her. Once she left, the keep and its residents would return to their lives, and soon, no one would think of her.

Chapter Fifteen

It took two days to prepare and pack, but they were blessed by clear and sunny weather as she and her maid and escorts rode out of the castle and through the village. Taking the road south along the loch, it would take at least five days of riding to reach her father's lands in the far south-west of Scotland.

She could not help her weakness as they made their way through the gate and soon, too soon, they were almost at the last cottage they would pass in the village. She turned to see if she could see him. He'd honoured her wishes. He had not come to say goodbye.

And part of her wished he had not paid heed to her words.

'My lady!' a voice called out before they'd ridden much further. Glynnis turned to see the baker's wife running towards them, basket in hand. 'Before ye go!' she called out, waving at her. They stopped and waited for her to reach them.

'Jeannie, are you well?' The woman, no young

lass, stopped next to Glynnis's horse and took in several breaths before speaking.

'I am, my lady. This is for you,' she said, handing up the basket to Glynnis. The aroma revealed the contents before she lifted even a corner.

''Tis very kind of you, Jeannie. Please thank Finley as well,' she said.

''Tweren't my idea or his, my lady. Iain stopped and asked for the loaves. Said ye hadna broken yer fast and would get hungry later. There's a crock of butter for ye, too.'

Iain knew she hadn't eaten this morn.

Iain...

'Weel, I didna mean to stop yer journey. Go on wi' ye now while the sun is shining and the roads are even,' the woman said. Glynnis tucked the basket's handle under her arm and fought the urge to search for one more glimpse of him. As she touched the horse's sides, Jeannie called out, 'May God bring ye back to us, my lady!'

She managed to hold back the tears until they were well away from Achnacarry. Until she lifted the edge of the cloth protecting the still-warm loaves of bread. They flowed until Maggie took the basket for fear the bread would be soggy before Glynnis shared it with her.

Iain had been watching. Even if she could not see him, he would watch her leave...again.

Robert Cameron turned to his wife, Elizabeth, as they stood on the battlements watching her goddaughter's departure. Tears flowed down her face at the last view of the lass and her escorts. Elizabeth did not cry often. The strongest woman he'd ever known, she had overcome so many terrible experiences in her life and come out without bitterness.

'I cannot believe it is the same woman leaving here today as the one who arrived a few months ago,' he said, taking her hand. 'That is due to your care, my love.' Kissing her hand, he stepped closer and kissed her cheek. 'She will always be grateful for your help.'

'But you were opposed to my bringing her here,' she said. Narrowing her gaze, she studied him.

'Aye, I made no secret of how I felt about it. Especially the manner in which you accomplished it.'

'Behind your back?'

'Aye. Without my knowledge.'

'You would have refused permission.'

'Mayhap I would have,' he said. 'Or mayhap I would have welcomed her openly. We will never ken.'

'Robert, I am sorry.' She leaned against him and he held her, because he liked having her close and they'd been too busy to be together much these last weeks.

'I ken.' Robert looked over the walls for any sign of Iain. 'Have you seen the lad?'

'Nay, not this morn. Glynnis said only that he would not be seeing her off.' Elizabeth stepped away from him and he missed her warmth immediately. 'I do need to tell you something.'

'About Glynnis?'

'Her father.'

Regretting the distance between them, Robert revealed his truth first.

'Worry not over her father. I sent him a letter telling him that any delays in her return were my doing. Blamed it on the Mackintoshes, which will give him something to think on.' She blinked in confusion. He wanted to laugh, for it was seldom that he knew something his wife did not. 'He tired of waiting for your response, so he sent letters to Glynnis and to me.'

'Why, Robert? Why protect her when you wanted nothing to do with it?'

'Because 'tis my duty to protect you, Wife. I will never allow any man to attack you again, even with his words, without answering it. Even when you do not think I ken what you are doing.' She lifted up on her toes to kiss him now and Robert liked it.

'And now?' she asked. Though he wanted to suggest they retire to their chambers to recover from the last weeks' endeavours with some *endeavours* of their own, he knew she referred to Iain and Glynnis.

'Your delay gave them the chance to reconcile to the truth of their lives. They owe you thanks for your meddling, but they will not realise it for some time.' He kissed her on the forehead. ''Twas your purpose? To give them time together?'

'Aye. If they could not be together, I wanted them at peace.'

His wife wanted them together, even if her words did not admit it to him. And, even now, she knew more than she had revealed to him. Gazing at her, Robert wondered if she was at peace with the way this had ended. He still stared at her when she spoke.

'And you, Husband? Did my meddling help you?'

'Aye, Wife. I was worried over the weakness she presented to him,' he said. 'I told them both my feelings on the matter and waited to see them make their choices.'

'Glynnis has no choices,' Elizabeth said. 'She must go where her father demands.'

'I think you underestimate her. And that surprises me since you are her biggest supporter. Without her sense of honour and loyalty, she could have made Iain miserable. Yet, look. She is on her way to carry out her familial duties and Iain is here. According to his words this morn, he is at peace and ready to arrange the betrothal visit.'

'So, all is well in your world, Husband?'

'Oh, nay, I would never be so foolish to say that. At the least not aloud so that my words tempt the fates against us.' He took her hand and led her to the steps, deciding that seeking their chamber was exactly what they both needed…together. 'But I just have a feeling that things will work out for the best.'

When he'd discovered Elizabeth's plans, he'd thought to put a stop to them, but one look at the young woman and he knew she would not survive if he sent her away. In spite of the inherent dangers of allowing the two to be back in each other's company, Robert had decided to let it play out. But not without making his concerns clear to Iain.

He'd told the lad the truth—he did not trust Iain's commitment to their plans. Now, though, tested and proven honourable, Robert could feel more confident about the arrangements after speaking in full candour to his tanist.

There was still much to be done before the Welsh *Princess* arrived, but all would be well.

All would be well.

Chapter Sixteen

Iain watched for the exact instant when Tomas realised he'd been defeated…again. Letting out a loud laugh, Iain nodded and held his cup up to salute his betrothed.

'You have done it again, Elen,' he said.

'You do not have to find it so amusing, Iain,' his cousin grumbled. 'I do not see you playing against her.'

'I ken my limits and that…' he pointed to the board now empty of carved pieces '…is beyond mine.'

'Is it true that you made the pieces?' Elen asked.

She held one of them—the red one designated as the queen—in her hand and examined it. He waited to see if she would run her fingers over the curves and flat surfaces and was relieved when she did not. His betrothed was more intrigued with jewellery and fine silks than carvings of common wood.

'He is quite skilled in carving wood and making

things. Why have you not told your betrothed about it, Iain?'

'Lady Elen appreciates the finer things in her life, Tomas. Wooden chess pieces hold no appeal to her.' His words were spoken without malice or insult intended and she accepted them as such.

'Except when I use them to defeat your cousin, my love,' Elen said.

They all laughed and Tomas took his leave to seek out less challenging company. As a servant filled their cups—costly wine that had been a gift from her father—Iain studied her.

From head to toe, beginning to end, the Lady Elen *verch* Pwyll was a complete surprise to him. Taller than most women, her head reached past his shoulders. Her wild, long tresses of black hair refused all efforts to be tamed, so she wore it loose around her shoulders, sometimes with a circlet or other jewelled decorations on it. Intelligence shone brightly in her deep blue eyes and her other features were quite pleasing.

But the element of her that he most liked was her absolute sense of honesty. 'Twas shocking in some ways to deal with a person who did not evade, dissemble or give the answer that was expected and was not true, even if it was the polite thing to say. Some took her behaviour as insolence or insulting, allowed only because of her being kin of the King, but Iain liked that about her.

He liked her.

'I did not mean an insult to your work, Iain.' She picked up two of the wooden pieces and looked at them more closely. 'They are fine work.' She placed them back on the board and began arranging the other pieces into lines with her graceful hands.

He tilted his head, acknowledging the compliment. She sat back after finishing arranging the game pieces and tossed her head. The movement caused her hair to cascade down her body—some of it flowed over her slender neck, some down across her full breasts, and it all pooled in a black cloud around her hips. The crooked smile that graced her bow-shaped lips told him she'd done it a-purpose and saw his gaze on her. Elen leaned closer to him.

'I would ask you about something,' she said. Glancing around them, she waited until the servants moved away. 'Would you tell me about her?'

'Her?' Iain looked around to see if Elen was watching someone nearby.

'The one they compare me to.' As he searched for a reply among his shocked senses, she shook her head. 'Come now, Iain. We both understand how this all works. And neither of us is a fool or a dim-witted child. We play this game of kings and nobles, as they move us like their pawns.' Her hand waved over the game board. 'But we had both lived our lives before they chose us to pull in like puppets.'

'Elen—'

'I have shocked you, but you know I speak the truth.' Elen slid forward on her chair until their knees met. In a bold move, she lay her hand on his leg. 'Tell me of her.'

'I—' He stopped. What should he say?

'I do not wish to be the centre of their gossip without knowing what, whom, I battle. Did you love her?'

'Elen,' he said.

'Iain,' she said, matching his tone. 'You told me there would be honesty between us.' Why had he said that? 'I know I am not what you or they expected. An outsider. I do not speak the language of the household well. I am welcomed, but not yet welcome. I am bold and I intimidate many,' she said, sliding her hand across his thigh. 'Tell me, so that I know the truth and do not have to believe the gossipmongers.'

She was correct about all of that. The household of Robert Cameron had been through wars and worse and were tightly knit together. Outsiders did struggle. As his betrothed, it was his duty to help her. Still, talking about Glynnis was not something he wanted to do with her.

'So, 'tis true then? You loved this woman?' Elen's tone was calm.

'Aye. I did.'

Elen nodded. 'Tell me of her.'

'Glynnis is Lady Elizabeth's goddaughter. She fostered here, planning originally to marry Robbie.' Elen had met Sheena and knew some of their story. 'We became close. We were young and had no idea of what the future would bring us.' He smiled, remembering their innocent faith in love. 'She visited here some months ago.'

'And I am nothing like her?'

Iain laughed. 'How am I to answer that, my lady?'

'With the truth?' He heard a vulnerability in her voice he'd not noticed before.

'Nay, Elen. You are nothing like her. Sheena once referred to her as Lady Paragon MacVirtue.' He winced as he said it. 'But Glynnis had been raised from an early age to carry out the duties of the lady of the household. Trained to be the wife of a nobleman or chieftain,' he said. She could manage a household, its servants, family, and keep it running smoothly. 'And she was kind. To everyone.'

'Ah, I am not kind.' Elen let out a sigh. 'I become rude when I am nervous.' She stood as did he. 'I have been nervous.' Again, the sound of uncertainty in her voice touched him. In an instant, it was gone.

'Did you carve for her?' Her gaze moved to the board and pieces and back to his. From the intensity of her eyes, the answer meant more than he first thought. But he'd asked her for candour and he would give it.

'I did.' He did not look away as he spoke.

'Ah.' She looked away first and was silent. With a shrug, her smile returned and she walked a few steps away from him. Speaking over her shoulder she said, 'I loved someone.' Facing him, he saw the stark loss in her gaze. 'But now, we are pawns together, you and I, and we go where we are sent.' Her lips trembled this time as she smiled. 'I think we will suit, Iain Mackenzie Cameron. I think we will do this well.'

She did walk away then, her hips moving in a feminine rhythm that made her hair sway with each step and it drew the eye of every man in the hall. There was an earthy sensuality about her that would appeal to any man. Well, most men.

So, she was willing to put their pasts behind them

and move on—both of them having loved and lost.
Both of them giving themselves over to a bigger plan,
pursuing their own goals for their own reasons.

It sounded just like every noble marriage he knew
about.

As theirs would be.

'Iain.' He'd been standing there, staring at Elen as
she walked away, and never heard Robert's approach.

'I did not hear you, Robert,' he said.

'I suspect your attention lingered elsewhere,' he
said. 'She is a striking woman.' Iain nodded. 'I had
wanted to speak to you both, for I have received word
from the King.'

The Cameron had his full attention now.

'Apparently, he leaves Edinburgh ahead of his
planned departure, so your journey there will be postponed until next month,' he said. 'I have told Elizabeth, so if you can share the news with Elen?' Iain
nodded.

'I will seek her now so that she does not prepare
without need.'

Tilting his head at Robert, he waited to be dis-
missed before following the path she'd taken through
the hall and out the doors to the yard. He heard her
laughter before he saw her—standing by the fence at
Tomas's side, watching the men training. Iain walked
towards them and realised that they were not just observing the fighting.

They were betting on the winners of each set of
men fighting in the yard. From the pained yell of his
cousin, Elen had indeed beaten him again. As he approached, they called out to him.

'Iain, your cousin has lost to me again,' Elen said, clearly enjoying every moment of Tomas's defeat.

'I may never show my face if she continues to best me in all manner of contests,' Tomas said. 'I may have to challenge her to a duel to save my honour.' He bowed, ceremoniously swirling his hand several times to her.

'Can you wield a sword?' Iain asked her. Her cheeks were flushed with joy at the little game she'd played with Tomas. She liked being challenged and given a chance to prove her superior knowledge or skills. Her eyes flared widely and she winked at him. 'Tomas, for your own welfare, I pray you withdraw before she accepts.'

Their banter continued until Tomas did leave the field, leaving Elen to him. He held out his arm to her and she slid hers around his, tucking up close to him. The fullness of her breasts rested against his arm.

'Will you walk with me to the village?'

'Is everything as it should be?' she asked after nodding.

'Some news from the King,' he said. He waited for her to ask, but surprisingly she remained silent as they passed through the gates and made their way along the road that led to Davidh's house.

He stopped in front of the stone house that was larger than the others in the village. The house given to the chieftain's commander, it had been his home once his mother moved back here, seeking the chance for her son to know his father's people. His original home here at Achnacarry was another of the bits of knowledge about him he'd not shared with Elen yet.

The cottage above the falls on the road leading north from the village had been the first place they'd stayed all those years ago.

He should tell her of that.

'Are we going inside?' she asked, releasing his arm.

'Nay. This way.'

He led her around the house to the large, enclosed garden that he thought had tempted his mother more than his stepfather had—at first. Pushing open the gate, he held it as she entered.

Being autumn, the garden had passed its full growing season and was filled with only the flowers' colour, herbs and plants that lasted into the cooler months. His mother would harvest and dry these last blooms for medicinal purposes. Iain walked to the place where the brightest of the flowers still blossoming were and picked one. Giving it to Elen, he took her hand in his and walked with her to one of the benches placed in the shade of the trees that grew around the perimeter of the garden.

'What is this?' Elen asked. Holding it close to her nose, she sniffed at it. 'The scent is lovely.'

'It is…a wildflower that grows here?'

'Oh, Iain, even growing up with your mother, you know nothing more than that?' Elen laughed at him and he decided he liked the sound of it. 'She spent her time here and you spent yours where?'

'Working in the stables. Working with the carpenters. Finally training with the other men,' he explained. 'I was just happy to be among my father's kin.'

'So, tell me of your claim to the high seat of the Camerons? The claims of my family back to the Great

Llewelyn are a bit convoluted. I confess, I did not pay
heed to all the details outlined in the agreement.' He'd
thought she would ask of the King's message and yet
she avoided the subject.

'It was a clear path when my father lived,' he said.
'He was the son of the chieftain Euan and named
tanist as a young man.'

'Ah. As father does, so does son.'

'Aye. If the lineage is direct, 'tis quite simple. But
my father was murdered before I was born. Before he
kenned of me.' He knew she'd been told of his birth
and that his claim came through being the natural
son of a previous heir.

'And your great-uncle Robert became chieftain.'

Iain laughed, for his route was a bit more confus-
ing than that and based on his cousin's decision to
step aside and not lay claim. 'I think we have more
in common than you might think, Elen. But after his
other brother was discovered to be a traitor to the clan,
aye, Robert became chieftain.'

She inhaled the scent of the flower and they sat in
silence for a short time. Unusual for them, but Iain did
not feel the need to talk. Finally, she let out a breath.

'Is there a reason you are avoiding the King's news?'
he asked.

'Anything from the King means he's meddling
again.' Iain could not help but laugh at the disgrun-
tled tone of her voice. Most would never admit being
vexed by the King of Scotland, but Lady Elen *verch*
Pwyll had no such qualms. 'I am ready. What changes
has he wrought in my life now?'

'Our trip to Edinburgh is postponed for some weeks at his orders.'

'There is more?'

'Only that his own plans to leave the city have changed and so ours are now to wait on his return.' She did not offer a reply. 'Is there something wrong?'

'I asked you about the woman in your past,' she said, looking at him. 'You should have asked me about the man.'

Chapter Seventeen

He liked her even more now. After her shocking disclosure about the reasons she was chosen to be given in marriage to him, to his clan, Iain felt less beholden and more at peace with his betrothed. Of course, learning the truth—that she'd tried to escape a previous arranged marriage by running away with the man she loved—gave even the fair-minded Robert pause. For a moment before anger filled his chieftain's expression, he thought Robert might cast up his supper. The insult offered to The Cameron and his clan and status replaced any softer reaction.

Davidh stood in the shadows of the chamber and said nothing other than asking a few questions. Struan answered Robert's call and Iain did not remember either older man having been caught unaware like this before. But a betrothal arranged by the King to his kinswoman made most men ignore any warning signs. The King had proved himself to be like so many common men who would hide their family troubles by foisting them off on someone unsuspecting.

'The lady suggested…the lady suggested I press the matter with the King? That I demand more now that we are aware of the true motives behind his agreement?' Robert asked. Lady Elen had shown herself to be extremely pragmatic in this situation. Robert shook his head before putting the heels of his hands over his eyes.

'My lord,' Struan said. 'She…ahem…the lady has a point. If this becomes kenned among our allies and, God forbid, our enemies, it puts us in a disadvantageous position.' Struan sat at the table and drank deeply from his cup.

'Why would the King risk such a thing?' Robert dropped his arms and joined the steward in the next cup.

'Because of me,' Iain admitted. The other three faced him, stunned by his words. 'I am the natural son of a man who was murdered before he could claim me. Not holding a direct line to the chieftainship, I claim it by your good graces and the acquiescence of my cousins,' he said, looking at Robert. 'A tenuous connection for a man who has no business calling out the questionable past of the betrothed given him by the King.'

'Davidh? This is not under your purview, but what advice do you have to offer?' Robert asked.

'Iain, do you have cause or desire to call out this deception—for that is what has happened—publicly?'

'None. But this is not my decision.' Strange how

he realised that truth as he said it. In order to achieve what he wanted, others made the choices for him.

'Will you hold ill will against the lass?' Davidh asked.

'Nay. I ken her part in this. She told me the whole of it.' A young man and a younger woman, in love, and making mistakes because of that love.

'I will think on this more and I will speak to the lady before making any decisions, but I see no good outcome for any exposure for either of you or the Clan Cameron.'

The discussion was over, yet Iain had a feeling that it was not done. Even in Elen's honest appraisal and explanation, her words made him think that there was more going on in the background with the King and her family than possibly she was privy to or knowledgeable about.

It would take some time to sort out and Iain was not certain he would like what they found, even if it meant large concessions from the King.

The next morning, after speaking to Elen, Robert confirmed his decision to go through with the arrangement. At the same time, he would send word to his factor in Edinburgh to push for some additional concessions from the King in light of this new disclosure. Since Robert would not reveal the source of it to the man, his representative to the King could rightly claim no knowledge of it.

Though Elen claimed to have been looking forward to visiting the city, Iain was glad to not travel there. He thought that the keep was nigh to unbearable when all those living within the household were caught inside on the worst of wintry days. His few visits to Edinburgh had left him feeling even more crowded and cramped.

Very few in Achnacarry even had knowledge that anything between them was awry, so in the eyes of the clan, the betrothal moved ahead with the marriage being arranged after the harvest, later in October. There was little doubt that the King would avoid the ceremony and would instead send someone to represent him.

None of that mattered to Iain.

He liked the woman who would be his wife. The honesty they'd already pledged to each other had kept his clan from being humiliated by the King. She laughed and made him laugh. He could find no fault and had no objection to taking her in marriage.

But, in the dark of night, 'twas Glynnis that came to him in his dreams. Glynnis he thought of when he woke. Glynnis to whom he compared every word and action that Elen said or did. She would never be Glynnis and he knew he must leave her behind if he was to be fair to Elen.

So he would.

Glynnis stopped for what felt like the hundredth time that day to seek out the privacy of the bushes along the road. If the men she'd hired to take her north had any issues with her strange pace of travel or her need to stop frequently, her gold coins had eased them. The stablemaster on her father's estate had found them—his two cousins—and sworn to her safety. Married to her mother's maidservant, the man had always held Glynnis in high regard and agreed to help her arrange this journey. Though he'd counselled her about the dangers in such a trip, she could not take the chance of putting into writing the concern that she must face. Thus far, his arrangements had worked out and his men had proven to be capable and steady.

Glancing up at the sky, she tried to estimate how many more hours they could ride before stopping for the night. She needed to arrive in Achnacarry while Iain was in Edinburgh with his betrothed to seek out the clear-headed advice of her godmother. She had no one else to ask and little time so she'd made arrangements to leave her father under cover of night before he could stop her.

'At least two more hours, if ye can ride, my lady,' one of the men called out after seeing her stare at the sky.

'Very well,' she said as the other man helped her back on to her horse. 'Let us try.'

They made it past Tor Castle without being noticed or challenged. Finding a place to camp just outside a small village, Glynnis knew she would not sleep as she waited for the morn and the final hours on the road.

But fall into sleep she had, for she woke as she'd been doing these last weeks.

Kneeling over, emptying her belly on the ground.

The older man held out a cup to her and she rinsed her mouth out and spat in the grass. Sitting back on her heels, she waited for the worst of it to pass. Each morn was different—the only constant was the heaving. Travelling on the boat from the south had been horrible and between the sickness that struck her when she was on the water and this one caused by her condition, there were times when she thought she might die.

This morn was nowhere near as bad as that, but it seemed unwilling to ease. Just when she thought it done, it hit again. Several more bouts of distress happened before she was able to get off her knees.

Mayhap the dread and anticipation of finally arriving in Achnacarry made it worsen? Mayhap the length of the journey affected it? Though each time she'd carried before had been different, this sickness had eased after only a few weeks.

It took nigh on two hours for her to be able to mount her horse and the clouds grew thick and dark in the skies above as they rode to the place where they would leave this main path and head inland towards Achnacarry. If she could manage to stay on her horse, they could be there by midday.

Pray God, she could!

The threatening storm did little to ease those last few hours on the road. Winds whipped up off the loch and riding, indeed staying upright, was a challenge. Somehow, though, the winds soothed her. Glynnis closed her eyes and allowed them to buffet her until their little group turned and headed west once more and away from the loch. They passed familiar places and slowed as the first cottage came into view.

Pulling her cloak around her and her hood up, she

and her escorts made their way along the main road towards the castle. Her plan was to enter and go directly to the keep and seek Elizabeth. Since Iain was not here, it mattered not that she was seen, and by the time he returned she would be gone and her godmother could concoct a story about her visit.

The path rose there, up to the gates, and they drew to a stop because of people riding out.

Iain was riding out. Her gaze took in the beautiful woman on the horse next to his. Everyone stopped and she tried to find words to say. From the shocked expression on his face, he was at a loss as well. It was the beautiful woman—his betrothed?—who finally spoke, breaking the tension.

'Iain? Who is this?' she asked. Then, after meeting her gaze and turning to the still-silent, still-staring Iain, she smiled and nodded. 'Welcome back to Achnacarry, Lady Glynnis.'

'My thanks,' she said, nodding back. 'I am looking for Lady Elizabeth.'

'She was in her solar when we left her, Glynnis.' He tripped over her name. 'Welcome back.'

She touched her heels to the horse's sides and guided the animal past them. The men escorting her followed.

She wanted to look back at him, but her stomach was roiling and panic was rising that she would be seen being sick. She heard the moment they rode on, listening to the hearty laughter from his betrothed as the need to heave grew. Glynnis turned her mount towards the stables and slid from her horse as soon as possible. Trying not to be noticed as her belly emptied was a valiant goal and not one she was certain she'd reached.

Someone had seen her. Luck was with her for it was one of the lady's maids who helped her to her feet and led her inside. Within a shorter time than she'd thought possible, Glynnis sat in one of the comfortable chairs in the lady's solar waiting as the maid sought out her lady to bring her to Glynnis. Though it shouldn't have surprised her that Anna would be the first person to arrive, it did. She'd not mentioned the healer as the servant brought her here, but Elizabeth trained her servants well.

'Lady Glynnis,' she said. She turned to close the door behind her. Coming closer, she said, 'Forbia said the lady's guest was taken ill. I did not ken you were visiting.'

'Elizabeth is not expecting me, Anna. I just need to talk with her. I need her counsel and then I can…go.'

Anna opened her mouth, but closed it without saying a word or asking any of the myriad questions she must have. On her arm was her ever-present basket of bandages and various herbs. This was her smaller collection since her workroom was just below and easy to reach for whatever she might need.

That workroom. That night.

'Are you ill, my lady? You were very pale and just flushed red. A fever mayhap?' Anna pulled a stool over closer to where she sat and reached out to touch her cheek.

''Tis not a fever, Anna. There is no need.' Glynnis nodded at the healer's raised hand and shook her head.

Glynnis leaned back against the chair and sank

into the thick cushions. Closing her eyes, she whispered the words she could barely say or hear without pain. 'I do not understand how it happened. They told me I could not. They told me this was not possible—and it may yet not be. They—'

'Who told you, my lady?'

'The Campbell's healer and several midwives who attended me. After the two were lost in the first months and the third was born too early and died… After I nearly bled to death, they told me it would not be possible.' Anna let out a loud and angry huff of breath. The woman's warm hands surrounded Glynnis's chilled ones.

'You told me only of the last one. I did not ken about the others. How far along might you be this time?'

She could not look at the woman as she spoke the words.

'Three months, two days and six or so hours along.'

Though she was silent, Glynnis knew Anna was not stupid. She missed little if anything that happened around her. But how could she speak to the woman who was carrying her son's child that he did not know about? To a woman who'd never had the chance to tell her own lover of his child. Before they were forced to say another word, her godmother arrived.

'Glynnis? Forbia told me you had arrived.' Elizabeth rushed to her side. 'Is she ill?' she asked Anna.

'I feel ill, but am not, my lady.' She began to stand until the lady waved her back down. 'I am sorry I could not send word to you. After your last letter saying that Iain was leaving for Edinburgh two days ago, I had to take the only chance I could to leave my father's house to get here to speak to you.'

'But Iain did not leave… Oh,' Elizabeth said.

'I saw him at the gate.' Now Elizabeth and Anna exchanged glances. 'Aye, with his betrothed. Lady Elen? They were leaving.'

'To greet Arabella as she arrives here. His aunt is coming to meet—' Another sentence interrupted.

'To meet his betrothed, I am certain,' she said. 'I pray you to be at ease of this. I ken he is betrothed. I ken his family would want to meet her before there is a public celebration.' She let out a sigh. 'I just did not think to see him here. Lady, truly I tried to avoid it,' she said to Elizabeth. 'I had no one else to ask for advice. For help.'

She felt the shivers before she understood what was happening. Her whole body erupted in tremors and the need to empty her empty belly struck again. The sight of the two women leaning in closer and talking about her grew hazy and dark.

'Lady Glynnis,' Anna said. Anna tapping Glynnis's cheek seemed to hold the darkness at bay. A warm blanket covered her and her body's shaking eased from its heat. 'She is exhausted, my lady. Travelling in this condition could not be easy. She should rest and I will fix a tisane to help settle her stomach so she can keep down some soup.'

'I agree,' Lady Elizabeth said. 'Forbia, ready a chamber for my goddaughter—' She stopped and pointed at the lass. 'And spread no gossip about this. I want no rumours spreading from you.' The servant's eyes grew wider and wider until Glynnis thought the girl might faint dead away.

'Aye, my lady.'

'Forbia?' Glynnis called to the maid. 'My thanks for your help today.' The girl smiled and curtsied to her lady and left.

'And then? After I rest?' she asked. 'There is more you need to ken about my father's marriage plans for me. It could not have taken my father very long to discover I am gone and he will ken where I have headed, my lady.'

'Rest. Drink Anna's concoctions. Then we can talk about what you must do or must not once you feel stronger.' Her godmother paused and tapped her finger to her lips. 'I must come up with something to tell Robert about your presence here.'

'A last visit to my godmother before marrying?' Glynnis asked. It was the ready excuse she'd used already along the way.

'Perfect for my use then since it is based on truth.' She stepped back. 'Anna, could you escort Glynnis to her chamber when it's ready?'

'Aye. I will go to my workroom to make what I need and return in a short time. Glynnis, rest here until I do.' Anna left, leaving only Glynnis and her godmother in the solar.

'I did not mean to cause upheaval in your life again, Lady.' The exhaustion struck her and her whole body felt as though she was covered by large rocks weighing her down. 'My father told me of the marriage he'd arranged just days after I realised...after I realised...' She succumbed to exhaustion.

* * *

The next time she opened her eyes, she lay ensconced in a warm bed with a thickly stuffed mattress and layers and layers of blankets. She remembered not how she got there or when. A glance at the shuttered window revealed it was yet day. The sounds from the corridor told her those living in the keep were still busy. She did not recognise this chamber as she pushed up on her elbows to look around.

Someone had hung the few gowns and other garments she'd brought on pegs or neatly piled them on a small table below the others. The leather sack of her things lay there, too.

Only at that second did she realise that she'd abandoned the men who'd escorted her without a word. If her belongings were here, they must have turned them over to Lady Elizabeth or one of her servants. That someone would see to their needs of food and drink comforted her a bit. It was how things were done here at Achnacarry.

A soft knock was the only warning before the latch lifted and the door opened.

'My lady?' Anna. 'May I come in?'

Glynnis pushed herself up to sit, waiting for the terrible rolling and twisting in her belly—which did not happen. Pulling the sheet up to cover her shift, she gave permission.

'Well, you look much better.' Anna checked the cups sitting on the table next to the bed.

'How long have I slept?' Gathering the length of her hair in her hands, she ran her fingers through the tangles before weaving a rough braid that would be sufficient for now.

'You arrived before noon and it's now just before sunset,' Anna said. 'The men who brought you said it's been a difficult journey for you. Sick at sea for days. Sick while riding the last miles. You scared them this morn.'

'I did?' They'd given no sign of being concerned about her during the journey… But they had. In their own way, both of them had helped her, sometimes before or without her asking for it.

'Men tend to avoid anything that has to do with crying women or womanly ills.' Anna sat on the bed's edge. 'So, the tisane worked?'

'Anna, I remember it not.' She searched her memories and the last coherent thought she had was in the lady's solar. 'How did I even get here? Or get in bed?'

'I do not doubt that. Forbia and one of the other maids helped in getting you settled here. Would you like to dress or wash?' Anna stood and reached for a clean gown. 'Supper will begin shortly and you might feel better up and moving.'

Accepting her help, Glynnis slid from under the bedcovers. She stopped and looked at the woman whose grandchild was now, tenuously, in Glynnis's belly.

'Anna, why? Why are you not barraging me with questions? Or demanding I tell Iain?'

'I did not realise I was carrying Iain when I saw Malcolm for the last time.' Anna paused for a moment, staring off, lost in her thoughts. 'But my mother did. Euan, his father, the chieftain, kenned that we were in love and I was a danger to his plans. So, he threatened my mother to make her leave and take me away. We moved when I was only three months along.'

Anna sat again, once more staring at the wall. Three months—the same amount of time since she'd been with Iain.

'Lady, I had my mother and her kin to support me during that terrifying time. I was young and scared. The women on Mackenzie lands took me in, made me welcome and helped me learn to be a mother while my own taught me to be a healer.'

Anna met her gaze now.

'You have no mother in truth. No kin to support you in this dangerous time for you. Your only support is Lady Elizabeth and you have risked all to get here to seek advice. How could I add to the burden and fears weighing you down?' Without being asked, Anna walked to Glynnis and began lacing up the gown. 'I have an opinion to give when you wish to hear it. If you wish to.'

'And Iain?'

'Well, I have an opinion about him as well that I will give you when you are ready.' Smoothing the garment down, Anna walked around her until she faced her. 'Will you join us at table?'

'Nay. They ken I am here, but my presence will disturb too many people.'

'He's asked about you already.'

'We are friends. I would ask after him.' She said it a bit forcefully, hoping she could accept that explanation, too. 'I will walk a bit while everyone is at supper.'

'Lady Elizabeth will send up a tray if you can eat?'
Anna looked at her for a response. Glynnis nodded.
'Soup? Bread?' She nodded again. Anna refilled the
cup on the table and poured a bit of something from
the little bottle there. 'Sip this before you sleep tonight. It should help to ease your belly in the morn.'

Once Anna left, Glynnis pulled on her stockings
and shoes and found her shawl. Her hair was less than
perfect, but since everyone would be busy with the
meal, no one would see her or notice. Going down
the stairs and taking the door that the servants used,
she walked into the yard and stopped.

The stormy and threatening day had turned into
a glorious one. The sunset, spreading golds and reds
against the blue sky, reminded her how beautiful
it could be here. After breathing in the air cleaned
by the rains, she walked towards the training yard.
Empty and quiet, she lost herself in her thoughts.

The one thing, the one that would make it easier
to take any decision would be knowing if she would
carry this bairn to birth. So far, she had no idea.
They'd spoken of damage and an inability to have
a babe. Even conceiving a bairn would not be possible, they'd counselled. Their words were not given
as guesses but as facts, so she thought herself unable.
Clearly, they'd been wrong about that.

Mayhap they were wrong about the rest?

She walked around the fence, kicking at stones
as she went. The doors to the keep were open and
a cheer went up inside. Tempted to go to the hall,
Glynnis decided that she should not. Now that Lady
Elen was here…

How could she tell him? How could she take away his dreams and the life he'd create when she knew not if she would lose this bairn as she had the other three? And there'd been so much bleeding the last time, the healer said she'd almost died. So, take away his chance at happiness when she could promise him… nothing?

Nay. She could not do that to him. She loved him too much to tear his life apart on something that might disappear on the morrow. The only way she would know the outcome would be to wait and by that time he would have married the King's kin. Nay. She could not tell him.

When she looked up, he was standing in front of her. Seeing him, she understood that she'd made her decision.

She could not tell him.

Chapter Eighteen

'I was on my way to the hall when I saw you out here.' That was partially a lie, but she did not need to know it. 'Are you not coming to supper?'

At that exact moment she moved into a stream of the setting sun's light and it surrounded her. Her hair shone in colours he did not usually see—golds and auburns—as she turned to face him. Her colour was better than the grim pallor in her face when she'd arrived.

'Nay.' She shook her head. 'I am not hungry.' As she pulled her shawl tighter around her shoulders, he thought she looked thinner than the last time he'd seen her. Her gown hung loosely on her body as though too big for her size. 'I would not like to encourage my stomach to rebel once more and repeat what happened just over there when I arrived.' Glynnis lifted a hand and pointed off near the fence closest to the stables.

'You travelled by boat?' Large or small, smooth surface or waves, it mattered not. Glynnis's stomach could not abide the movement on water.

'You remember?' she asked. Before he could laugh at what they both remembered, she spoke. 'I am still truly and heartily sorry for that.'

He'd assumed, since her family was from the coastal lands, that she was accustomed to travel by boat. In spite of her warnings, they'd gone out on the loch in a fisherman's boat and…his best boots had been the victim.

'Your mother has given me something to settle my distress.' She touched her hand to her stomach. 'Not the most horrid of her treatments at least.'

'What brings you here, Glynnis?' From the shocked look on her pale face this morn, she had not expected him to be here. So, she must have been in contact with Lady Elizabeth before the change in the plan to go to Edinburgh.

She did not speak at once. She was considering her words and from the small telling movements of her teeth on her lips and her shifting gaze, he knew she was about to lie to him.

'My father gave me permission to visit my god-mother one last time before I travel to his estate in England for my marriage.' He did not expect that. And now, he could not tell if it was the truth.

'England?' She would move to England and he'd never see her again. If she spoke the truth.

'Aye. He has arranged a marriage to one of the noblemen with an estate bordering on ours. He, William, is in need of a wife.'

'And so you will go.' It was not a question truly for the sad smile and shrug she made reminded him that women, that she, did not have the right to object. 'I do wish you well, Glynnis. I—' What else could he say?

They both carried out the duties expected of them and they would go separately about their lives. When he looked at her, he could see she struggled.

'Are you certain you will not join us at table?'

'That does not seem a good thing to do. I will upset the company and make things awkward.' True and yet he did not want her to disappear without another word to him. Selfish, he knew, but he could not help himself on that.

'She seems lovely, Iain.' The compliment sounded sincere, but he would expect nothing less from her.

'She is.' He heard the little, short intake of breath and knew he'd surprised her. As he'd been surprised that he did like Elen. 'Elen is not what anyone expected.'

The laugh she uttered sounded sad.

'Iain, I thought you would be away. I did not plan to see you and upset your arrangements,' she said softly. And yet he was glad to see her again, whatever the reason.

'The King changed his plans, so we changed ours,' he explained without saying more. Robert wanted to keep the knowledge of the rest of the debacle in the making to a very small number.

Cheers erupted in the hall and echoed across the yard to them, reminding him where he should be. He stared at her, taking in what could be his last look, before nodding his farewell and walking back to the keep. He glanced back and noticed that the sun had dropped and no longer illuminated her. But he would remember her as he'd seen her.

Reaching the steps, he climbed them and entered the hall. The main table was filling with those closest to the chieftain and he took his place with Elen beside him and Tomas to her other side. He kept a watch on the open door, hoping that Glynnis would walk through it and join them.

But, in the end, she made the most sensible decision and did not attend the meal.

Glynnis kept to the shadows, entering below-stairs and coming up the stairway that led to the tower. Standing there, in a small alcove that hid her from view, she watched him.

Watched them.

Lady Elen was a stunning woman. She laughed often and well and managed to draw Iain into it. Glynnis wished that his face could have softened and lit with enjoyment for her. But it was not meant to be. The lady was bold, sitting close to him and placing her hand on him as they ate and spoke. She and Elen were as different as night and day in their temperament and behaviour.

From here, she could see that Iain did like her.

Though her heart hurt, she was glad he would have someone not afraid to show her emotions before others. Someone who would bring joy into his life.

'He looks more and more like his father with each passing year.' The soft voice startled her, for standing where she was, no one should have been aware of her.

'My lady,' Glynnis said, nodding to Iain's aunt.

Arabella Cameron was known as the kindest, most beautiful and gracious lady in the Highlands and Glynnis had tried to emulate her behaviour. 'Is The Mackintosh with you?' Glancing at the table, she did not see him.

'Nay. I wanted to meet the woman Iain will marry but without all the ceremony that seems to happen when he arrives.' Lady Mackintosh laughed. 'I wanted to be informal and get a chance to speak to her. To find out more about her.'

'She seems lovely, though I have only been introduced to her,' she said.

'She has a sense of humour and I think that will be good for him.'

Glynnis just nodded, growing unable to speak for fear her voice or words would give away her true feelings.

'Elizabeth told me you'd been unwell. Are you feeling better?' the lady asked.

'I am. The journey was hard and I do not travel well on water,' Glynnis said, covering her stomach with her hand.

'Many of us do not travel well.' Arabella turned to Glynnis. 'Elizabeth has asked me to offer you counsel on some private matter. She said you needed help and advice? But I will not step into where my words are not welcome.'

Glynnis almost laughed aloud at the lie. The Mackintosh complained often about how his wife loved nothing better than meddling and manipulating those around her. And that, since how much she intruded was commensurate with how much she cared, he was forced to allow it to continue.

Had Elizabeth told her the truth? Was she meddling because it involved her beloved nephew?

'You are looking peaked, Glynnis. Seek your bed and rest. We can speak on the morrow if you wish it.' Glynnis lowered her head respectfully when Iain's aunt took hold of her hands and pulled her close. 'You still love him?'

'I do. Against all sense of pride and common wisdom, I do.'

The admission slipped out without hesitation. The lady looked as if she had something else to say and chose not to.

'Get some rest.'

Then she was gone, as silently as she'd arrived. Glynnis left the alcove and sought her chamber.

A tray awaited her, with a bowl of broth and some bread, as Anna had promised. Though not hungry, Glynnis ate it, dipping the bread into the soup and chewing it. Her stomach seemed soothed, but she sipped the cup as she undressed and readied for bed.

She fell asleep with her hands on her belly, praying for so many things.

One hundred.

Then to two hundred.

When she'd counted up to three hundred and had not heaved yet, Glynnis chanced sitting up. The grey light of dawn barely lit the chamber, but she'd placed a basin on the floor if needed. Had Anna's potion worked? Sliding her legs from under the blankets, she waited.

It hit as soon as her feet touched the floor.

This morn's bout of distress passed more quickly than others had. Mayhap the tisane had eased it? Or mayhap sleeping in a warm, comfortable bed and resting well had?

After her ablutions and dressing, Glynnis made her way to the solar to await the lady's arrival. Avoiding the hall, she found the chamber empty. Walking around it, she found a tapestry she'd worked on years ago and which was now complete. She'd embroidered the red flowers since she'd liked that colour best when they were choosing what they would each work on. Sliding her fingers along the piece where it hung on the wall away from the hearth, she could still find Sheena's stitches along several of the flower stems.

Sheena hated sewing and anything that meant using a needle. Many times in order to help her friend, Glynnis had tucked in rows of stitching when Lady Elizabeth left the chamber. The lady must have noticed them, but chose not to remark on the clear differences. Glynnis had tried to help Sheena prepare to marry Robbie and eventually be lady of the household. As she grew to know her better, it quickly became apparent that Sheena's limitations would never allow that.

The sounds of voices approaching down the corridor warned her that it was time to come to a decision. Well, she'd made that choice—

'Good morn,' the lady's maid said as she opened the door to let her mistress into the solar.

'Good day, Forbia.'

Lady Elizabeth entered along with Anna. The Lady Mackintosh followed them into the solar. It was clear to her that they had already been discussing her and her situation before arriving here in the chamber. With barely a tilt of her head, her godmother sent the maid out, leaving the four of them alone.

'Did you sleep well, lady?' Anna asked. 'I've brought you something different to drink than the one from yesterday. Still soothing to your stomach, but a bit lighter and refreshing.' She carried a kettle and set it near the hearth. ''Tis good hot, but I prefer it at a tepid temperature.'

'Whichever you think best,' Glynnis said. Anna poured it into a cup and handed it to her. 'And, aye, I slept well.'

'And the other?'

Glynnis glanced around to see if Iain's aunt was listening. From the knowing glint in her eyes when she'd entered, the lady had already guessed or been apprised of her condition. 'Better this morn.'

'I do sometimes think you are a witch, Anna,' Lady Arabella said. 'Your potions and concoctions certainly are more successful than any our healer makes.'

Anna's mother had been rumoured to be 'the Witch of Caig Falls' because of her skills in healing. Iain had told Glynnis that his mother had inherited that calling and some had called her that as well when they first lived above the falls.

'Lady, as I have told you many times, there are no such things as witches. Only wise women.'

Everyone grew serious, knowing that the time for truth had come. The women each found a place to sit and Glynnis spoke.

'First, I have decided that I cannot tell Iain about my condition.' She expected arguments and lectures, tirades even, so the silence surprised her. The older women exchanged glances that spoke of prior discussions without her.

'You do not expect to carry the bairn to birth then?' Anna asked. She'd heard what Glynnis had never said but feared.

''Tis not happened yet. The first ones did not last this long. They said that I would not conceive let alone bear a child due to the damage within me. I cannot hope when it has been burned out of my heart and my soul.'

'Iain should ken,' Anna said.

'He is happy, Anna. You ken how hard he has worked to attain this. His betrothed is here and the marriage approaches. I cannot tell him and ask him to wait. The King will brook no delays in his plans. Especially not for Iain to wait to see if his former lover carries his child. Which matters not in the King's plans. And it is likely a child who will not be born.'

The silence again was unexpected. Tears trickled at first and then flowed.

'I cannot... I will not ruin his life by telling him I'm carrying and then break his heart and disappoint him when I fail again. I thought I would never recover from my loss before, but that, disappointing

him, failing *him*, will be something I cannot survive.'
She looked at each of the women and saw their tears.

'Is that how you think my son will react to this news?'

'Nay. He will be what he is—kind and caring. He will postpone the marriage and face the ire of the King if I ask him. Then, his wife-to-be will grow resentful that he has chosen me over her and if, at the sad eventual end of it, they marry, it will taint their marriage from the beginning of it.'

She stood up and walked to the table to put the cup down.

'Do you not see how many lives will be ruined if I tell him?'

'Glynnis, I think—'

'Nay, Godmother. I have made my decision.'

'And now what?' Lady Arabella asked. 'What will you do? Go back to your father and accept whatever marriage he makes for you?'

Glynnis slumped into the chair. All her confidence—it was all a charade. 'If I return to my father, I will have no choice.'

'Travelling back at this time is not wise. It might bring about the very thing you seek to avoid,' Anna said.

'What will you do?' Iain's aunt asked once more.

'I do not have a plan.'

All of her strength left her then and the overwhelming sense of failure and despair filled her. She had no plan. No way out of this that did not include returning to her father, empty and barren.

There was no good ending to this, she understood

that. Lady Elizabeth could not be seen to be helping her thwart the wishes and plans of her husband and the King. She could send word to her father that she was ill and would return when she was able, but he was yet furious with her lady godmother over the delay in Glynnis's return home at his call. What she'd told Iain was true—he had a marriage arranged with an English nobleman. A return home meant leaving Scotland for the rest of her life.

'I still think you should tell my nephew.'

Glynnis looked up and saw that Arabella Cameron wore a strange expression on her face. It made Glynnis remember Brodie Mackintosh's comment that his wife was happiest when meddling in someone else's affairs. And the lady looked ready and willing to meddle right now.

'And I think Iain should ken,' Anna added.

'As do I,' Lady Elizabeth said.

Glynnis clenched her teeth together and shook her head.

'If you are determined to wait it out, what then? You will bear a child out of wedlock? Or you will return to your father when the bairn is well established within you and pass it off as your husband's?'

Glynnis winced at that path. It would seem that The Mackintosh's wife would ask all the challenging questions this morn. 'I am willing to do that. To raise his child on my own. I am already widowed and would not be the first to have a child without a husband if I must.'

Anna came to her and knelt down in front of her. 'If you do this, if you give birth to Iain's child and do not tell him, it will greatly disappoint him when he discovers your deception. He will remember that his father never kenned of him and the regrets that have filled his life over that. But where this differs is that when it happened to him, it was not within my control to do otherwise. This time, this time, it *is* in yours.' Anna took her hand. 'And he will grow to hate you.' Glynnis flinched at such a thought.

The sobs escaped her at the truth of the words. Her decision would ripple out in directions she'd never thought of. In wanting it to be her choice, she'd made a bad one.

'Elizabeth. Anna,' Lady Arabella interrupted then. 'Glynnis is trying to make a decision when there is not a good one to make and too much pressure will result in a bad one,' Arabella said. 'I have a suggestion. An invitation.'

'What do you have in mind, Arabella?' Lady Elizabeth asked.

'Take another day to rest and then bid farewell to us here to return with your escorts to your father. But once away from the village, you will travel instead back to Glenlui. It is a short journey. One you can make comfortably well. I will send word to make the arrangements for your stay and let my husband know.'

'Will he agree?' Lady Elizabeth asked that question. Allowing Glynnis to recuperate here had caused trouble between her and the chieftain and she worried that it might happen with Arabella.

'Brodie has never liked men who bully women, whether wives or daughters or sisters. He will allow you refuge. If I remind him of a debt he owes me, it will work out.'

'This will give you about six more weeks since the wedding is planned for after the harvest is brought in and some winter preparations done,' Lady Elizabeth added. 'If all is well, you would be—'

'Four months, two weeks, three days,' she and Anna said together. That the woman remembered almost the exact number was unexpected.

'That will give you a better idea if the pregnancy is strong enough to continue,' Anna said. 'I think that your shock over your husband's accident and death brought on your labour too soon. If you make it through these early months, there is a good chance of...'

The chamber quieted as they each thought on this offer and what it would mean. In her heart and soul, Glynnis feared it was all for naught, but these good women were giving her a chance. Even though they disagreed with her choice.

'And you all still think I should tell him now?'

'Aye.' Their voices spoke the word in unison.

'Will you tell him if I do not?'

No one spoke and Glynnis felt the helplessness of never having a choice settle on her. Once more a pawn, but now to these women instead of her father.

'Nay,' Anna whispered.

'Nay,' her godmother said softly.

'Not I,' Iain's aunt said. 'Not that I would not want to, but this must be your choice.'

'My thanks,' she said. 'I owe Lady Elizabeth such

a debt of honour and now I owe you each one. I swear
I will find a way to pay it back.'

They spoke of details and arrangements to be
made and explanations to be given for some time
before each going in a different direction to make
ready to carry out this plan. She dared not hope for
the best outcome, partly because she did not know
what that would be and partly because she could not
hope. But she wanted to. She wanted to hope.

Glynnis did as Arabella had suggested and rested
as much as she could that day. When Elizabeth asked
her to join them for dinner, she could not refuse.

Even if it meant spending time with Iain and the
woman he would marry.

Chapter Nineteen

Iain was surprised to see Glynnis walking to the table for their evening meal. Though he'd seen her a few times through the day and she did appear to be feeling better, he suspected that she would avoid sharing meals to prevent an awkwardness among the family.

He was not the only one surprised as Robert's hesitant greeting showed. The chieftain had not expected her presence either, but he made her welcome. The seating had been changed and the table seemed split by age—with his mother and stepfather down at one end with Robert and Elizabeth, Struan and a few of the elders, while he and Elen were placed at the other end with Tomas and Glynnis sitting nearest to Lady Arabella and Lady Elizabeth.

Tomas had become Elen's biggest supporter though he demonstrated it by relentlessly teasing her. Elen bore up well and gave as good as she received, whether to a jest or a game. Into that volatility Glynnis entered. Though the first part of the gathering felt tense, through the meal, things eased and the conversation grew comfortable as they spoke of Tomas's childhood and his antics with his brothers, Robbie and Alan. Tomas could tell a story well.

Soon, the table was cleared by the servants, leaving only pitchers and cups for them and he thought everyone would leave. Instead, everyone but Struan remained.

'Tell me of your home, Lady Elen,' Glynnis said. Through every exchange she had been gracious to the woman at his side. 'I have travelled little and not outside Scotland.'

'It can be a lovely place,' Elen said. 'But mostly it is hills and glens and rivers and the sea. And castles. Ruled by England's Child King and his minions while many Welsh princes yet plan uprisings.'

Iain looked around at those who had heard her description and the reactions were diverse. From his father's shock to Glynnis's studying gaze, Elen had done what she liked to do—spring surprises on others in her words and actions. But she was not a mean person and did it more for her amusement than to attack or humble another.

'As did the mountains of Scotland before we threw off the yoke of English rule,' Iain said.

Cups were raised and the praises of The Bruce called out. The Camerons and most of their allies had come out for Robert the Bruce and so supported the efforts for re-establishing a sovereign Scotland.

The conversation continued and one by one, or couple by couple, the rest left until only he and Elen and Glynnis remained. He wanted to ask about her visit here, but she would not speak of such things in front of Elen. When she stood to leave, he did as well.

'You leave in the morn?' he asked.

Robert had briefly mentioned her plans to him earlier. This visit did not seem to cause the same strife between him and Lady Elizabeth as her first one did, so he did not pry.

'Aye,' she said. The smile she wore now was the mask she used when she was nervous. Or did not wish to speak about something.

'I hope your journey is less trying than the one here was,' Elen said. 'Iain told me of your weakness on boats. Your path home can be on land?'

'It will take longer, but, aye, I will avoid the water on the way back.'

He wanted to say more, but they were, as Elen had described them, puppets being pulled. That included Glynnis. If things had been different, he would… He stopped himself.

'I will seek my chambers,' Elen said, standing and making her way down the steps from the dais on which the table sat. 'I will see you on the morrow, Iain. Do not forget you have promised to take me to the cottage where you lived as a child.'

Elen was gone before he could speak, but he saw the wink she gave him as she turned away. She knew he wanted to speak to Glynnis. And she was giving him this opportunity.

'Did I chase her away?' Glynnis asked.

'Nay. Elen—' He stopped and shrugged. 'Elen does as Elen does.' His betrothed knew he loved

Glynnis and had left them alone to say their fare-wells now as they each understood what they faced.

'Your betrothed is lovely, Iain. I like her. She will keep your life filled with laughter.' Glynnis smiled. 'And I think she will surprise you.'

He knew that to be true so far since she'd arrived. Elen hid some extraordinary qualities as well as undoubtedly some secrets it would take him years to discover.

'She has already,' he said. 'You are well enough to travel back? You were exhausted on your arrival.'

He could not help himself. He walked to her and took her hand in his. Tangling their fingers, he brought her hand to his mouth and kissed the back of it.

'You must have a care. And send word to me if you have need of me.' She paled at his words and he shook his head. 'I mean that I remain your friend and would help if you need something.'

'I must go, Iain.'

He released her and watched as she walked away.

He'd thought he was ready to give her up. That when they parted those months ago, he could walk away without regrets.

Seeing her again, unexpectedly, had shown him that he was a fool. And watching her leave now, knowing she was lying about something, telling him what she thought he needed to hear instead of what he should hear, made him want to drag her away and keep her until she told him the truth.

But doing that would hurt her. It would make it nigh to impossible for her to continue to hold on to the sense of peace she had about another marriage.

They'd separate that night and if she did not ask for his help, he would honour her wishes.

And let her go…again.

She watched from a short distance away—far enough not to be noticed in the shadows and close enough to see and hear them. Elen knew that no one thought she had a softer side, but she did. The loss of the man she loved had torn her heart out. Iain's quiet acceptance of her foibles and bad manners and boldness had eased the pain she carried and made her believe they would get along well.

Elen could never love him, and from what she'd witnessed between Iain and Glynnis, he would not welcome her love.

Did they think they fooled anyone? Or mayhap because she was an outsider, she noticed it? The attraction between the two was scorching—like standing too close to the hearth when it was ablaze. From what she'd overheard, they had each accepted the arrangements of their parent or lord and left each other behind to do as they'd promised.

But their hearts had remained bound together.

Elen watched as Glynnis left the table then, making her way to the guest chamber she'd been given for her stay. Even from her place, Elen could see Iain's thoughts on his face.

He wanted to claim Glynnis. To stop her from leaving. Keep her as his own. But she had learned one critical thing about Iain Mackenzie Cameron since her arrival—he stood by his word. Even when she'd revealed some of her own shame to him.

She'd done it because she liked him and wanted to protect him and his kin from the danger of the King's machinations. He'd been one of the first men who'd treated her with respect and kindness even when he knew more about her. Telling him the truth was the least she could do.

Elen listened to the sound of his boots as he walked out of the great hall and towards the tower where the family's chambers were. She would wait here for a bit to let him reach his room before going to hers. She'd just moved along the corridor that led to the stairs when a twinge of guilt made her pause.

She had not been completely honest with him and neither had Lady Glynnis.

Again, she could not be the only one to see what was right before them. Well, some of them—Iain's aunt, Lady Elizabeth—already knew the truth. The men never saw things about women unless it involved bedding them, so she could understand why they missed it. Elen had not.

Over and over during supper, the lady had touched or covered her belly.

Not because her stomach was bothered by travelling in a boat, which seemed to be the excuse she was using. Nay, just like most every other woman carrying a child did, Lady Glynnis touched the place where a babe grew within her. Many of times she witnessed it, Elen noticed the lady looked longingly at Iain as she did it.

Yet, just now, when she'd given them the perfect chance to speak of things privately, neither one did.

So, although Glynnis was carrying his child, Iain did not know.

Walking on, she wondered why Glynnis had not revealed it and planned to return to her father and enter a marriage he'd arranged. She turned the corner just in time to see Iain enter his chambers. Making her way silently, she reached her door when it struck her.

Glynnis was not going to her father. The lady was running…somewhere.

Elen wished she could cheer the lady on, since they were like-minded and clear in their purpose. For once her own marriage was accomplished, Elen was leaving. With the protection of his name, she could set out on the search she must make. Without anyone to follow or watch her. She might be too late, but unless she tried, she would never know.

Lifting the latch, she entered her chamber and waved the serving maid out. Once she was alone, she wondered about her reasons for not exposing Lady Glynnis. Part of her, the angry part she kept hidden deeply, the part that had been subjected to mean, vicious acts of humiliation by others, wanted to.

Her time here had forced her to remember that there were good people. People who cared. People who were kind. People who treated her well.

Iain was one.

Glynnis was another. She remembered seeing her as they each recognised the other's place in Iain's life. Unlike most women, Glynnis had been pleasant. Each time they met she had spoken to her as if she mattered. Never a bad word or tone that insulted her.

So, Elen had done the same. Iain and Glynnis had been in love. And been lovers. But Elen had no doubt in Iain's ability to remain faithful to her if he pledged that to her.

She blew out the candles and climbed into bed, knowing she'd made the right decision about them. Even if Iain did not know of Glynnis's condition yet, their secret was safer with her than hers was with those who knew it.

Chapter Twenty

Ten days later...

The cottage was larger than the one in Achnacarry. And it was in the middle of the village rather than hidden away in the forest. Lady Arabella visited her most days after her return from Achnacarry as did several of the other women in her household—Rob Mackintosh's wife, Eva, and her daughter, Arabella's daughter Joanna, who was almost the same age as Eva's, along with cousins and villagers.

Rob's sister Margaret, who worked as their healer, brought her several tonics and such, and though they were not Anna's, she drank them down. The occasional bleeding that had happened before ceased and the stomach distress eased with each day. Only one of her pregnancies had made it this far along, so she was uncertain if those were good signs or bad.

She did miss Maggie, whom she had left at her father's home, and hoped the lass had not suffered too much at his hands. She had not confided in her at all, so she could not be blamed. Mayhap she would send word to her once this was all sorted out and Maggie could join her wherever she settled.

Had word reached her father from The Mackintosh yet? When she arrived, he and his steward had been waiting for her. True to his wife's word, the powerful chieftain of the Chattan Confederacy treated her kindly. Until he told her otherwise, Glynnis would consider herself his guest and under his protection.

'Good day!' Margaret called as she entered. 'Are ye ready for our walk?'

One of the first things Margaret had insisted on was that Glynnis not sit inside and wait for something—good or bad—to happen. She believed that keeping busy was important, so she knocked on the door almost every day and asked her to come along. Not a young woman at nigh on two score years, but she had the bearing and attitudes of someone much younger.

Part of that was due to having the strong, big, braw Magnus as her husband, Margaret said. Magnus winked at her over his wife's head as she said it. Each day, as they walked along the paths and visited any number of villagers, Margaret shared another story about the feud between the Mackintoshes and Camerons and how it had ended.

'Hiv ye broken yer fast yet?' Margaret looked around for evidence.

'I had a bit of bread and cheese,' Glynnis said. Finding her shawl and the basket she carried along on their outings, she faced the stern taskmaster of a woman and answered the rest of her questions.

'Did ye keep it in yer belly?' At her nod, the woman

continued on. 'Ah, 'tis good. Any sign of bleeding? Did ye sleep? Are yer feet swelling?' It took about a quarter of an hour to go through all of her questions before she was satisfied and they could leave.

Lying in bed just before she fell asleep was the worst time of the day. That was when all her doubts and longings came roaring out, keeping her tossing in her bed until weariness pushed her to sleep.

Yet, in the light of day, she was confident in her decision. To unnecessarily force Iain to change his marriage arrangements and create more problems was not the right path to take. They could not be together, so let him move on.

One morning, as she rolled on to her stomach to sleep a bit longer, she felt it.

A movement so slight she thought it was her imagination

Then it happened again. 'Twas like the fluttering of a butterfly's wings within her. She lay perfectly still waiting for it, but it was done. Turning over, she placed her hands on the slight bump now there and waited to feel something.

The first two times, she never got to…four months, so only once had she experienced this. Torn between the joy of it and the possible loss she faced, she remained abed. Margaret did not come to her door, so she stayed under the covers until her needs forced her out. The morning turned stormy outside, but there in the cocoon of her warm bed, she fell back asleep and dreamed of a wee lass with blue eyes that matched her father's.

And ten days after that...

Iain rode through the forest and along the loch like the very devil was on his heels. The winds tore at his face and pulled his hair free of its binding. He'd not returned here since, well, since he'd been here with Glynnis, but the need for some time alone had built to such a strong need he could not ignore it any longer.

When he arrived at the turning place near the loch's edge, he slowed the horse and guided it down the smaller path. Soon they reached his shieling and he slid down to the ground. Tossing the reins over a tree that bordered a patch of grass, he went inside.

Of course, nothing had been moved or changed. He doubted anyone knew about this place, other than Glynnis, and if anyone did, they would not bother it. He took out his flint and worked a piece of straw until it caught fire. Lighting the lanterns, he leaned up against the main worktable.

He picked up a square wooden block from the crate where he kept pieces at the ready and turned it over and over in his hands. Many times, he carved without a plan, not knowing what animal or creature was buried within the wood. Only after he began cutting away chunks did the shape appear. A few times, he consciously decided what to make, but those were less often than the other way.

His fingers itched and he picked up the first of the chipping knives to take off the largest unneeded chunks. Using the mallet, he continued chipping and then whittling the smaller bits away. His hands moved without him deciding anything, and some time later, the perfect replica of the fisherman's boat formed in his grasp.

Clearing away the dust and excess from the table's surface, he placed the flat-bottomed boat there.

And then the laughter erupted from him.

No matter what he planned or thought or avoided, she crept into his thoughts. These last weeks since she'd returned home, he'd tried to work out why she'd lied to him that day. Even with the privacy Elen had given them, Glynnis had revealed nothing to him.

When she left, he should have been able to bring his full attention to his forthcoming marriage. But Elen was keeping something from him as well. Oh, she did not taunt him with it, but it was there in her ice-blue gaze when they were together. The day he took her to Caig Falls and showed her the way to the top and to the cottage where his grandmother had first been called 'the Witch of Caig Falls', she'd wandered around the gardens planted there and she'd started to speak to him several times before stopping and walking away.

Secrets would out. That was a fact and it had happened in his life. His identity was one held only by his mother on their arrival here. She'd wanted to accomplish a promise she'd made when she received the news his father was dead and her return to his kin was part of her larger plan. He'd laughed at the irony that he was now fulfilling that plan with his marriage and position as tanist.

Smoothing the rough edges and planes of the boat took a little time and then Iain was ready to go back to Achnacarry. The tension within him settled as did

the recognition that he must clear up any friction between him and Elen. If they were marrying soon, he
wanted it gone.

He tucked the boat in his sporran and put out the
lanterns.

Iain arrived back at the keep and went in search of
Elen. Finding her in the solar, sitting in a corner away
from the other women, he asked her to walk with him.
They made their way up the tower to the entrance
to the battlements. Walking along the heights of the
keep, he drew her to his side. When he faced her, he
found a puzzling look in her eyes.

'Is something wrong, Elen?'

'I think there is,' she said. Before he could ask,
she spoke. 'Have you decided to break the betrothal
then?' She stepped back and crossed her arms over
her chest.

So there was more going on. Reasons he would
not like. From the way she clenched her teeth and
her body tensed, it was not good.

'I have not,' he said. 'Is there some reason I
should?'

She let out a breath and shook her head. 'You have
been different, moody, difficult since Glynnis left and
I thought you had changed your mind.'

'I have been grumpy,' he admitted. 'And after you
were kind enough to give us time to speak alone before she left.' He leaned in and kissed her forehead.
As she had before, she quickly tilted her face and
positioned it so that his lips met hers. She opened
to him and he kissed her deeply. Lifting his mouth

from hers, he nodded at her. 'I apologise for my sullen mood and difficult ways.'

They stood at the wall as people went about their duties below them.

'I just thought you must have found out the truth and were angry over it,' she said. Before he could ask, she placed her hand on his arm and went on. 'Iain, it would be acceptable to me if you wish to bring your child up in our household. It is not such a rare situation after all, not in Wales. And you have told me about not kenning your father, so I ken how important it is to you. I do not mind—'

'What?' He might have yelled the word for Elen startled and backed a step away from him. He took her arms and pulled her closer. 'What did you say?'

'I ken you still love her, but she will be a noblewoman alone with a bastard and it might be the kinder thing—'

'Stop!' He squeezed her arms. 'What are you speaking of? What child?'

Her face drained of all colour as she stared at him. 'I thought you kenned. Your... Someone must have told you that Glynnis carries your babe.'

Flashes of white and then red filled his sight. He released her and stumbled back.

'Glynnis cannot bear children. I ken you have withheld some of your own truths from me and offered lies in their stead, Elen. But why would you lie about her? About this?'

One look at her face and he knew she spoke the truth. Mayhap she did not know the whole of it, but what bits she did know were true.

'How did you find out?' he asked, pulling himself under control.

'I...um...I watched and put the pieces together. The two of you in love. Her arriving with a sickness that seemed worse in the mornings. Hearing the gossip among the servants and others when they did not ken I was listening. Then, there was the way she touched her belly while not taking her gaze off you.'

He shook his head. 'What way?' he asked. 'How did she touch her belly? Are you sure it was not just the stomach distress?' The words sounded foolish to him as he spoke them.

'Like a woman who is carrying touches her belly. A protective caress.' Elen's hand dropped down and slid across her own body in the movement he'd seen many, many times before. Sheena during her recent visit. Women in the village and keep, too.

'I did not see it,' he admitted. Shaking his head and shrugging, he met her gaze. 'I have been a fool.'

'Aye, you have been,' she said with no sound of jesting in her tone.

'And you have been more generous than most noblewomen would be. Even offering as you did,' he said. 'We must speak, but first I must find out the truth.'

He held out his hand to her. Iain did not wish to abandon her here.

'Go. Do what you must.' She turned away and looked over those moving about below. 'I suspect there will be no marriage between us when you return.'

Iain ran, passing the guards on duty, down the stairs and through the hall to the chamber Robert used. He pushed the door so hard, it banged on the wall and bounced back.

'Robert!' he shouted several times as he entered and he saw the chieftain reading a packet of letters Iain had not seen before. Robert jumped to his feet at Iain's call.

'What is it?'

Before he could reply, guards ran into the chamber, clearly responding to what they thought must be a threat to The Cameron. Iain leaned over with his hands on his thighs, trying to slow his breathing. 'All is well.' He shook his head at the guards.

Soon, Davidh rushed in, sword drawn and dagger in hand, with more guards at his back.

At least the protection of their chieftain was in good stead. It took several minutes to clear the room and Davidh looked as though he would argue to stay until Iain made it clear that the discussion was for Robert's ears only.

Robert poured two large servings of *uisge beatha* and handed one to Iain, waving him into one of the chairs. Both of them swallowed the liquid rather than savouring it and their cups were empty with two mouthfuls.

'I thought we were under attack, Iain. What is the matter?'

'Lady Elen just offered to raise my child—the one Glynnis now carries—in our household.'

Sucking in a chest full of air, Robert began coughing. Iain poured more liquor into their cups and waited until Robert could breathe. 'That was my reaction. Did you ken about this?'

'Nay! I kenned what brought her here, but I did not have any knowledge of a pregnancy.' Robert sipped this time. 'Wait a moment. Your child?' He emptied the cup. 'I did not ken.'

'I did.' They turned and found Lady Elizabeth standing in the doorway. Walking in, she closed the door behind her and stood there.

'Lady,' Iain said. 'Is she pregnant?'

'Aye.'

'And she returned to her father? Without telling me?'

'Nay, aye. I mean she did not tell you, but did not return to her father.'

'Elizabeth.' Robert leaned his head in his hands. 'Again? Again, you meddle in this?'

'So where is she if not returned to her father? I need to speak to her.'

Iain paced around the table until Robert grabbed him and made him stop. He knew before she spoke the name. Everyone was aware of his aunt's expertise in meddling where she saw fit.

'Arabella.'

'So is Glynnis at Glenlui?' If he left now, he could be there in a few hours. The lady nodded.

'Iain. Go carefully. You cannot seek entrance there the way you just did here. Gather your wits and your self-control and approach The Mackintosh in a calm manner. Ally or not, kin or not, he will not accept insults or threats to his wife.'

'I understand, my lord. After I speak to her, we must discuss Lady Elen and the marriage.' Iain would not be marrying anyone but Glynnis.

'Oh, we must that,' Robert said, pointing at the packet he'd been reading. 'There is news and some rather shocking concessions there.'

None of that mattered now. Now, he must get to Glenlui and find Glynnis.

It took him three hours. He left with the clothes on his back, a skin of water and a sack of oats in case he was delayed. The skies held and he made good time. The guards waved him in and he rode to the stable to give the horse into the care of the men there.

Directed into the hall, he found his aunt and uncle-by-marriage about to eat supper. The servants placed trays and bowls of food on the tables as he walked up to them. Climbing the steps up to their table.

'Iain?' The Mackintosh called out. 'Come, join us for supper.' From the height of their dais, Iain could look out over the whole of the hall and see those seated below. Studying those at tables and those walk-ing about, he could not see Glynnis.

'My thanks, Uncle, but I must find Glynnis.' He stood behind them now and leaned over towards his aunt. 'Just tell me where she is, Aunt.' When she re-mained silent, Brodie whispered something to her. Letting out a sigh, she looked up at him.

'I will not have her upset or bullied, Iain. Not by her father or even you.'

'Is that what you think I will do? I have only just learned that she carries my child. I need to speak to her.'

'Who told you?'

'Not one of those who should have. But my betrothed thought I kenned of Glynnis's condition and spoke about raising the child in our household.'

Brodie groaned aloud and his aunt had the sense to look ill at ease.

'In the cottage at the end of Margaret's path,' she said. 'She will be alone, so I pray you approach her cautiously.'

'No matter what has been told to you or should have been, the lady is under my protection, lad. See to it you respect that.'

'I love her, Uncle. I would do nothing to harm her.'

He knew where the healer lived. Rather than riding, he made his way there on foot. The sun was setting earlier now that autumn had arrived, so he did not dawdle along the way. Passing Margaret and Magnus's cottage, he walked along the path to the last one, a small cottage sitting by itself, and stopped before it.

His thoughts and what words to say jumbled in his head now that he was here. He knew he could never marry anyone but Glynnis. It truly had not taken the news of a bairn to make him realise the truth, but it had given him the kick he needed to do what he must do. As he'd thought on his responsibilities to his clan and to her, he understood he was not above using their child to make her see the path forward—together. She was his and would be only his.

What he did not know was why she would keep such news from him? Had she meant to have his child and not tell him? That did not feel like something she would do—not when she knew his own heritage and beginnings. But fear made people do unexpected things and that would explain much.

Well, he would never find out if all he did was stand and stare. Iain walked up to the door and knocked, not too hard nor too lightly.

'Glynnis?' he said. 'I need to speak with you.' He knocked once more. 'I pray you to open the door.'

Silence met his request. If she was asleep, would she hear him there? Tempted to lift the latch and enter, he was stopped by footsteps behind him. Turning, he found Glynnis watching him.

'All is well?' a man's voice asked from behind her.

'Aye, Magnus,' she called out. Margaret's husband must have walked her back to the cottage.

'Goodnight to ye.' The man walked off, leaving them alone.

'Glynnis.' And no other words came to mind as he stared at her. 'You look well.' She did. From what he could see in the shadows.

'Iain,' she said, walking past him to go inside. She stood with the door open, waiting for him to enter. He stepped within. Before she could close the door, a voice called out to her.

'Lady, is all well?' Robbie Mackintosh, the chieftain's cousin and commander of his warriors, stood there with his arms crossed over his chest. He must have passed his brother-by-marriage on the path here. Clearly, Brodie Mackintosh wanted Iain to understand the lengths he would go to in order to keep his order of protection. Glynnis stepped into the man's view and nodded.

'I am, Robbie.'

'I will be up the lane speaking with Magnus if you have need, Lady.'

The man walked away.

He waited to see if anyone else would happen along before following her inside. The cottage was a nice size, and from its appearance, it seemed that his aunt had assigned servants to see to Glynnis's needs. A fire lay ready to be lit in the hearth. The place was tidy. Iain watched her in silence as she began to light a few candles around the cottage.

Nothing in her shape or movement gave any indication of her condition. But she was only a few months along and mayhap it would take longer?

'Who told you?' she asked in a voice filled with a wearied tone. As though someone had broken a confidence. Which would explain the sense of disappointment even while it gave him a good idea of which women were involved.

'Can we sit?' he asked.

She chose a cushioned chair by the hearth, leaving him the bench next to the small table. She waited on his explanation while all he wanted was to take her in his arms and kiss the breath out of her.

'I am not certain if it will surprise you or not—'

'Elen?' He nodded. 'Your betrothed?' He shook his head. No matter what it took, that would end.

'Well, she was when she told me. Apparently, through her observations, overhearing of conversations not meant for her ears and her own best guesses, she realised that you were, are, carrying a child. She even offered to raise the child in our household when she thought I kenned your condition and was saddened that you would be raising the child on your own.' He moved over in front of her and crouched down before her. 'My child. Our child.'

'She is surprising and candid and…correct,' Glynnis said. 'For now.'

'What do you mean? You are pregnant?' He held his breath.

'You do not ken the whole of it, Iain,' she said, releasing a sad sigh. ''Tis most likely that I will lose this as I lost two more before the most recent one.'

The words were stated very calmly, but he heard the anguish in her voice and saw it in the way her shoulders began to droop and her body tucked itself down, preparing for the pain.

'Did you think I lied to you when you heard this?' she asked.

He shook his head. 'I thought only that it was a miracle. Unexpected. Unlikely. Tell me the rest of it, Glynnis. There were other losses?'

Over the next pain-filled minutes, she revealed the other bairns lost and the extent of the most recent damage that had made the midwives and healers and her believe she could not get or remain pregnant. But what he did not understand was why she thought she could keep it from him?

'Why did you not tell me? Did you think I would allow you to bear my child alone?'

'I do not think I will bear your child, Iain. This will end the way the others did and I cannot ask you to give up all you have worked for and dreamed of, what your mother struggled to give you the chance to earn when I ken—' She stopped and took in a breath.

'Any day now it will seep away and my failure will destroy your dreams and I could not bear to see the disappointment in your eyes. When I fail you.'

'Glynnis, you will not fail me. I want you, I want to marry you, regardless of whether you can bear children or not.'

'You say that now—'

'And I mean what I say!'

She reached out and covered his mouth with her fingers. 'You mean it now. But in a few months, when it ends as it will—'

'As it might,' he corrected, whispering around her fingers.

'As it will,' she said. 'If you believe my warning and reject what you have accepted as your destiny, you will tell yourself that you do not mind that you gave it up for me. But when I lose this bairn and the empty years stretch out before us, you will grow bitter. You will name me as the cause of your failure to be tanist and to lead your father's clan.' She began to cry, silent tears trickling down her cheeks. He knelt and tried to wipe them away.

'The worst part is that I ken the truth. And I would rather walk away from you now than watch our love decay from the banked resentment you will feel.'

From the desolation in her gaze, he could see it would be hard to convince her of his love for her, no matter if they had children or not. But he knew that if his father had had the chance to claim his mother's love, he would have given up titles or power for her. Malcolm Cameron had given her his most prized possession as a pledge of their love, intending to claim her. And he died never knowing of his son's existence.

He would not do the same. He would not give her up, come what may or may not. But he would have to convince her of that somehow.

He needed to show her that he loved her, not the bairn she carried. Right now, though, he'd surprised her and their conversation had exhausted her. Continuing would not convince her, so he would have to come up with a way to do that.

'I think I should go,' he said, standing and pulling her to her feet before him.

Leaning down, he kissed her. Not the way he wished to, but just to taste her and feel her in his arms. He nearly yelled when she opened to him and even more when she leaned her body against his. Sliding his hands along her arms, he held her tightly to him. The kiss changed and she took control of it. His body reacted to her touch, her taste, her nearness. He stepped away, holding on to her shoulders until she gained her balance.

'Tell me just one thing, Glynnis.' He walked to the door and turned back to her. 'Tell me the truth—do you still love me?'

'Iain,' she moaned out his name in protest.

'Elen told me you do. But I want to hear it from you. Do you love me?'

She did not speak for several long moments before nodding. 'Aye, Iain. Always.'

Iain held in the joy that filled him at her declaration. But he tempered it because that was just the first step in a longer process to convince her.

'I ken you were seeking a safe place here while you waited and I have disturbed you. I will be staying in the keep if you have need of me.'

He left her before he did anything foolish and walked down to the healer's cottage. After asking her to check in on Glynnis, he walked back to the keep with Robbie. He needed help if he was going to succeed and he knew the exact people who could help him.

His meddling Aunt Arabella and her powerful husband.

Chapter Twenty-One

Margaret arrived just after Iain left, bearing a calming tisane to help her sleep. The healer checked her without saying much other than that Iain had asked her to see to her.

In truth, once Glynnis had realised who stood there before the cottage, she'd had to fight off the urge to run to him and beg him to stay with her. Not seeing him would have made this easier, but now that she had, she admitted to herself that she would crave and accept every encounter she had with him.

If he had listened to her, he would soon be on his way back to Achnacarry to finalise his marriage arrangements with Lady Elen. As she rose this morning, the news that Elen had revealed her secret made her smile. She truly liked the woman—they could be friends if not for Iain. Intelligent. Candid. Funny. Kind. All traits she'd found in the Welsh noblewoman.

Glynnis had risen for the day, without illness, so she planned to walk to the well and bring fresh water back here. The servants Arabella had sent to her would, but Margaret had told her she would be away this morn for their usual walk and Glynnis liked to feel useful each day. Getting the smaller bucket, she opened her door…and found most of the villagers standing there.

Confused as to the reason, she watched as Iain, Brodie, Arabella and others walked up to her. Margaret and Magnus were there, too. And Robbie and his wife, Eva. Iain approached and held out his hand to her. It felt like more than a simple gesture and Glynnis hesitated. When she met his gaze, the love shining back at her almost brought her to her knees.

She took his hand.

'My lord, would you tell Glynnis what you did for me this morn?'

'Iain, what is this? Why is everyone here?' she whispered to him.

'I want no secrets between us now, Glynnis. I want my intentions known before witnesses.' He nodded at Brodie and waited.

'I sent a messenger as you requested to The Cameron to inform him that you have ended your betrothal to Lady Elen *verch* Pwyll,' The Mackintosh said on Iain's behalf.

'Iain! You cannot.'

'I have, Glynnis. 'Tis done. I had already told Robert before I came here so he kenned my intentions.'

'Why? Why give it up? Give her up and all she brings to your marriage?' Why could he not see the mistake he was making? She would be his downfall.

'Because, in spite of missteps and terrible timing and changes we could not control, I have never stopped loving you. All I tried to accomplish was because I could not have you. But given the choice, I would take you over all the rest. As I have come to realise that my father would have made the same choice all those years ago,' he said. His aunt stepped closer when he paused.

'Losing Iain's mother broke Malcolm's heart,' Lady Arabella said softly. 'I did not understand the cause until later in talking to his friend, but he loved her, as Iain loves you. I hope you will not make the same mistake and not take love when it is within your reach.'

Having others stand for him would not convince her that it could work for them. She knew it would not. Nothing would work out and she would be left empty and grieving again and Iain would be angry and bitter.

'I cannot, Iain. I cannot take the chance of such a loss again.'

'I will be at your side, no matter what happens, Glynnis. You will not be alone.'

'We will be here, too,' Margaret called out.

'Glynnis,' The Mackintosh said. 'I pledged my protection to you when you arrived at my wife's behest. And that stands. If you accept Iain's offer, you are both welcome here. If you naysay it, you still have a place here. You need never go back to your father's control.'

'How? How can you do that?' In spite of it being a serious question, a titter of laughter echoed through the crowd watching this all happen.

'I have allies and friends in high places,' he said. 'And a bit of experience in hiding people who wish to escape their situations.' Glynnis did not understand his meaning, but his kith and kin did and nodded in agreement. Vague memories of an heiress hiding from her father, who thought her dead, rose in her mind.

'Do you love me, Glynnis?'

She hesitated. Saying it to him last night when only the two of them heard it was different from declaring it here.

'I love you, Glynnis MacLachlan. Do you love me?'

'Aye,' she whispered.

'Weel, any fool could see 'tis the true,' someone called out and those observing this strange proposal laughed.

'Be my wife, Glynnis? As soon as The Mackintosh and my aunt can arrange it?' She heard his aunt's reaction and knew that instead of everything being set against them, in truth, everything was set up for them. 'Trust me, love. We will sort this out and be together always.'

When he said it like that, with so many offering their help and dozens more awaiting her answer, how could it be anything but…aye? Fear raced through her and panic controlled her for a brief moment as she wondered if it could possibly work out for her, for them.

'Steady on, lass,' he said. She smiled, remembering the last time he'd spoken those words to her. The workroom, right before they had their one night together. He rubbed the inside of her wrist, a soothing movement that calmed her racing heart.

'Steady on, Iain,' she whispered back. 'Aye, I will be your wife.'

The cheer went up and she was snatched away from Iain's grasp to be hugged by so many others. It took a while before Iain claimed her back and they went inside her cottage with a promise to come to the keep later to discuss *matters* and what must be done. When they did not leave fast enough to suit him, he actually closed the door in his uncle-by-marriage's very shocked face. Inside, he walked Glynnis to the bed.

'Come, I want to hold you,' he said, tugging the bedcovers down and climbing in fully clothed.

She stood and watched as he made himself comfortable and held out his hand to her, patting the bed next to him. Unsure what he planned, she waited.

'I spoke to Margaret and she said we should not risk consummating our marriage yet. So, I just want to hold you now. 'Tis been too long since that night.'

'Three months, three weeks, two days and about four hours.'

He looked at her and laughed. 'If anyone is counting.' Iain rolled to his side and pulled her close, their bodies touching. 'All will be well,' he whispered. Kissing her, she felt his love and believed him.

For the first time in so long, she felt hope spark in her heart.

Epilogue

Achnacarry Keep—five months, three weeks and a few days later...

Her back hurt.

Her belly hurt.

She wanted food.

She did not want food.

She wanted it over.

She wanted the pains to stop, but not yet.

She wanted the baby.

After trying desperately not to do anything that would make the bairn come, now everything was focused on bringing the bairn forth.

'Be ye ready, my lady?' Lorna asked. ''Tis time to push again.' The midwife was far too cheery for this situation, Glynnis thought.

'I was ready this morn,' she said, sharply. She remembered almost nothing about giving birth the last time, but she would remember every second this time. Anna and Margaret, who had travelled to Achnacarry to help, recommended not taking concoctions to help her bear the pains that might make her sleepy and her body less effective. Glynnis wished she'd not agreed with that now.

'She was ready weeks ago, Lorna,' Iain said from behind her. With her big unwieldy belly and swelling feet, Glynnis had not been comfortable and had not been quiet about it. She had a lot of apologies to make to those who'd spent time with her lately.

'Weel, the bairn be ready now,' Lorna said, leaning over and adjusting the sheets.

No one else was with them, but so many waited in the hall for word and to be close if they were needed. Glynnis and the baby had made it this far and she now had faith they would come through safely this time.

Iain had been at her side since he came to Glenlui to get her. Through every moment since, whether battling her father over their surprise marriage or worrying over the pains that had terrified her through the last months of the pregnancy, he was with her as he'd promised. And he stoked the hope that had begun that day when she trusted in his love.

With the next strong wave of pains, she could not think any more. Her body took over and worked to give birth to their miracle bairn.

Within two hours, the bairn was delivered safely, Iain had fallen in love with a lass other than her and they now waited for those below to meet the newest Cameron.

'Are you ready to meet them?' Iain whispered to

their daughter as he waited to hand her back to Glynnis. 'They are getting unruly out there.'

'They will ask about a name,' she said. Glynnis had refused to discuss names, fearing it would tempt fate to interfere. Now, they needed one.

'What do you think of Fiona?' Iain asked. ''Twas my father's mother's name.'

'I like that. We can come up with another after they meet her,' Glynnis said. Elizabeth would be a perfect middle name in honour of the woman who'd done so much for Glynnis in her time of need. But Fiona was a fine name for their daughter. Glynnis pushed herself back against the pillows and waited for Iain to let their family and friends in to celebrate the special gift they'd been given.

Against all hope. In spite of missteps and bad timing. Because she'd chosen Iain and his love.

On that same day, many miles away, in the hills of Wales, Tomas Cameron came face to face with the woman for whom he'd searched these last three months. It had taken weeks of negotiations between his father and the King's ministers to sort out all the scandalous issues involved, but Elen *verch* Pwyll had consented to marry him. And he'd agreed, for the sake of his clan, to take her as his wife.

Watching her surprise as he entered the cottage, he controlled the rage he'd carried on this journey. He wanted the truth and he would get it. She'd boasted of her candour when he first met her, but he'd had no warning of her deception.

It was one thing to be the youngest son and get

whatever his brothers cast off, but he never expected it to be a wife. And he'd never expected that that wife would put something in his ale on their wedding night that knocked him unconscious and made her escape possible.

But she had and she did and now she would answer for it.

* * * * *

If you enjoyed this book,
why not check out Terri Brisbin's story
in the Highland Alliances collection

The Highlander's Substitute Wife

And be sure to read her
A Highland Feuding miniseries

Stolen by the Highlander
The Highlander's Runaway Bride
Kidnapped by the Highland Rogue
Claiming His Highland Bride
A Healer for the Highlander
The Highlander's Inconvenient Bride

Author Note

This story very much focuses on the heroine's ability, or not, to provide an heir for her husband and touches on the very established view of the times—and even more recently—that a woman's value is tied to that. Wanting 'an heir and a spare', for example, continues in some societies even today.

All of that touches on both the infant/child and maternal mortality in those times. It's shocking, when researching medieval history, to discover that the infant/child mortality rate was between forty and sixty per cent. That most babies born did not reach puberty! That the first five years were the most dangerous and if they lived that long they had a better chance of survival. If a woman gave birth to four babies, chances were that two or three might not survive.

Of course, some of that depended on class and wealth and status, but those rates were not always better for nobles or royalty. Also, we know that being pregnant and giving birth was the most dangerous thing a woman could do in those times.

All of that gives us some background into the conflicts and motivation and challenges and fears that Lady Glynnis MacLachlan faces. Never fear, though, for as in any romance the love of a good man makes all the difference in the world to how things turn out.

And Iain Mackenzie Cameron *is* a good man.